THE WRONG WOMAN

An absolutely gripping crime mystery with a massive twist

HELEN H. DURRANT

Detectives Lennox & Wilde Thrillers Book 3

Joffe Books, London
www.joffebooks.com

First published in Great Britain in 2023

© Helen H. Durrant

ISBN: 978-1-80405-747-6

PROLOGUE

Adam Lansing tore at the sealed envelope, fingers trembling, the tension evident on his face. He looked at the young detective by his side, hot tears in his eyes. "What if this isn't the end? What if the kidnapper changes his mind? What if he doesn't give Lori back but simply demands more money?"

"Best not get ahead of ourselves," the detective advised. "For now we follow the instructions in that letter."

Adam knew he couldn't cope with more waiting, he was already a nervous wreck. "He said one payment would secure Lori's freedom, but will it? Can I really trust someone who's kidnapped my wife, who's held her captive this last week, taunting me with photos of the woman I love in pain and discomfort?" In normal circumstances, the answer would be a firm no, but right now, Adam was ready to grasp at anything that offered hope. "This lunatic could drain me dry and still kill Lori."

"We'll be at the drop-off point waiting," the detective assured Lansing, watching him stuff the banknotes into a sports holdall. "When he comes to pick up the money, we'll arrest him."

Lansing shook his head; there was still no guarantee. "He holds all the cards though, doesn't he? Arrest him and he may never say what he's done with my Lori."

One full week had passed since she'd disappeared. He'd held it together, told those who asked that she was away staying with family, that her father was ill. All except his friend and occasional golfing buddy, Anna Noble. He'd told her the truth and her advice was to go to the police. Was she right? Well, he couldn't keep the pretence up much longer, it was driving him mad.

The kidnapper promised that once the money was handed over, the ordeal would be finished. Adam had followed the kidnapper's instructions to the letter, but now, at the final hurdle, his nerve failed him. He needed help, and despite what the kidnapper had written, earlier today he'd taken Anna's advice and gone to the police.

He raised his worried eyes from the letter. "He writes that he'll contact me tomorrow with a time and a place. He promises to keep his end of the bargain but I must make sure I get my part right." He shook his head. "I'm beginning to wonder if contacting you was a good idea."

"You did the right thing," the detective assured him.

"So you say, but if anything happens to my Lori, I'll lay the blame at your feet."

"Don't worry, Mr Lansing, we have this now. It won't be long before your wife is back home."

He wished he could believe that, but the nagging doubt remained. "I hope you're right. All I can do is follow instructions and trust whoever is doing this to keep his part of the bargain."

He examined the single sheet of paper, looking one last time at the final sentence. He blinked away the tears, bringing them into sharp focus.

This will be over tomorrow. Before midday she will be returned to you.

CHAPTER ONE

Three weeks later

Monday

The sight was grisly, grotesque, so horrific it made DS Jess Wilde shiver. It wasn't the fact the woman was dead — after all, death and murder came with the job. It was the way the victim's face had been practically obliterated. That, and the fact that she'd been left dressed in old-fashioned clothing, made for an odd scene. At first glance, the victim's face appeared to be heavily made-up, but Dr Melanie Clarke, the pathologist, had already discovered that she was wearing a mask. A mask that gave their victim pale skin and red Cupid's bow lips, like those old Victorian dolls with heads of china that you see sometimes in antique shops. Her blonde hair, now thickly matted in blood, was done in ringlets with red ribbons that matched the colour of her lips. The entire effect was spooky, unnerving. Jess had seen nothing like it before.

DI Harry Lennox spoke in his familiar Scottish burr. "This entire scene shouts weird to me. I'm no expert in these things but she looks like an antique doll."

The victim was clothed in an ankle-length white dress which had ruffles across the chest and hung loose around the rest of her thin body. Her lower legs stuck out from below the frilled hem like sticks, showing black lace-up boots. Her skinny arms were folded over her chest.

Melanie joined them at the entrance to the tent. "The post-mortem will confirm it but right now I'd say her death was down to the beating she's taken to her head and face. Wasn't done here though. There's no blood or brain tissue on the ground around her."

Melanie's words made Jess feel slightly sick. She shivered again.

"The mask on her face is hiding the worst of what was done to her," Melanie continued. "Thoughtful of your killer, don't you think? Maybe he was aware that kids take a short-cut along here to Ryebridge High in the mornings and didn't want to upset any sensitive souls. Though as it happens, it was a group of them who found her and called it in. I'll know more about what they did to her once I get the body back to the Reid Centre and set to work. One thing I can say, the body is extremely cold and unusually thin. She might have been held somewhere in the cold and not fed. Or she may have had some sort of eating disorder."

This made Jess Wilde shudder again. "Poor lass. Is there anything on her to help us with identification?"

"Nothing yet, but something may turn up when we look at the clothing," Melanie said.

"Why is she so cold? It's more than rigor mortis, isn't it?" Jess said.

"It's possible she was killed some time ago and kept somewhere cold, a large fridge for example. There is a little decomposition but the flesh in question is abnormally cold too. That will muddy the waters in estimating when she died. But you know me." She smiled. "I'll do my best."

"Murder then," Harry stated.

Melanie gave him a quizzical look. "Oh yes, there's no doubt of that. You don't get those sorts of injuries by accident. Once we get her back, Hettie will look at those clothes and add her expertise to the mix. They might give us a clue to where she's been."

Jess bent to have a last look at the body before it was taken away to the morgue. "Poor girl, she is thin, you can even see her ribs sticking up through the fabric." She looked closer, squinting against the weak morning sun flooding in through the tent entrance. "The dress looks authentic. The bodice has lace panels and tiny mother-of-pearl buttons. I've got photos of some of my ancestors wearing gear like this. We should ask ourselves where the get-up came from if it really is the genuine article."

"How old is she?" Harry asked Melanie, who was now outside, organising the removal of the body.

"I'd put her at between twenty-five and thirty," she said, carefully placing the wig in an evidence bag. "Her real hair is short and dark. It also shows evidence of having been dyed not long ago. You can see the coloured streaks in it."

"Despite the clothing, very much a girl of today," Harry mused. He looked around at the immediate surroundings. "It's not exactly secluded here. Whoever dumped her was taking a risk."

"Ryebridge Park," Jess said. "But if she was put here in the early hours there wouldn't be anyone around."

"There are houses over there." Harry nodded.

"My own house is only a few hundred yards that way," Jess said. "But I doubt anyone living there saw anything, the trees obscure the view."

"It's still worth knocking on a few doors and making sure. I'll get Col to organise it." This was DC Colin Vance, the third member of their small team. "He can get some of the uniformed officers on it." He turned to Melanie. "You said kids found her."

"Yes, on their way to school."

"Are they okay?"

Melanie snorted. "Apparently kids from round here don't turn a hair at finding a dead body in the park. One of them rang the police. When they arrived, the kids were standing a short distance away, taking photos. Despite the bravado they obviously didn't get that close. They told that uniform over there that the most scary thing was the clothing. They've been told to keep all images off social media, but I can't promise anything."

Harry rolled his eyes at Jess. "We'll have to speak to them pronto, the school as well. I don't want her family finding out that way."

"I'll ask the uniform who dealt with them to sort it. There were three of them, apparently, and they were taken on to the school to give their statements."

Harry stood looking around at the immediate area. "Where do we start?"

"If Col does the door to door and the local traffic cameras, we can do missing persons," Jess said.

"We don't know that she was missing, but we'll give it a go. At this point in the case we need to try everything. Most important is giving the poor girl a name." He looked at Melanie. "Let me know right away if you find anything."

"We'll do our best but there's nothing in the pockets of the dress, so there's no mobile, I'm afraid."

"When will you do the autopsy?" Harry asked.

"This afternoon at two. I'll do the preliminary stuff when I get her back — X-rays and blood tests — so I should have something for you quite soon."

"See you later in that case." Harry smiled. None of them liked autopsies but given the job, they had little choice.

* * *

"I feel strong coffee calling, what about you?" Jess said.

Harry nodded and trailed after her to the waiting cars.

"I've not had a chance to ask, how's your new place?"

Until a few days ago Harry had been lodging with Jess. Her house was a new build, her first foray into homeowning and her pride and joy. She'd offered Harry the spare room because he was desperate for somewhere to live and the rent would help her with the bills. But Harry's untidiness and sloppy ways grated on her nerves, so much so that last weekend they'd had a blazing row and in a fit of pique he'd moved out.

The anger didn't last long. Harry was well aware of his shortcomings, and a couple of hours later he turned up on her doorstep with a huge bunch of blooms and an apology. He wasn't angling to come back, he said, he'd managed to get a place of his own sorted. A mate of Col's, Ryan, a Scottish bloke like him, had agreed to take him in for the time being.

"You do realise, don't you, that you're going to have to dive in and buy a place of your own sooner or later?" Jess said. "Think of it as an investment if nothing else. That little box of mine has made me several thousand and I've not been in two minutes."

Harry shrugged. That sounded too much like putting down roots to him, and he wasn't sure he was ready. Ryebridge was okay, but it wasn't home. What family he had left lived in Dunoon on the west coast of Scotland, along with all his old friends. He'd left out of necessity, running from a villain who wanted his blood. Him and a host of bad memories had forced Harry to make a quick exit from Scotland. Hopefully, he'd return one day. When that day came he didn't want having to sell a house holding him back.

"I'll think about it," he said.

"No you won't, you're afraid. It's written all over your face. I can read you like a book, Harry Lennox. You're hankering after moving on, aren't you?"

He shrugged. "One day, perhaps."

CHAPTER TWO

A mug of strong coffee later, the pair got down to work. Harry briefed his small team, DC Colin Vance and two uniformed officers, while Jess made a start on the missing person records.

"Do I concentrate on Ryebridge or look at the whole of Greater Manchester?" she asked. "Only if I do that, given her age group, we're looking at a lot of missing women."

"Ryebridge for now," Harry said.

"Any hints about timescale? Kept in a fridge is the popular opinion, and you know what that means."

Indeed he did. The poor woman could have been dead for a while. "Given we're keeping it local, start recent and work back in time. Get a list from the last three months and we'll look at them first."

A reasonable plan as far as looking for a needle in a haystack went. For now, it was anyone's call. She was about to comment when Colin interrupted.

"There aren't any traffic cameras by the park," he said. "But the main road into that area has a couple. If the body was dumped early this morning, we should spot something. Uniforms have got nothing from the door to door so far, but they'll try again when people get home from work."

An hour later and despite their best efforts, the team still had very little to go on. Jess had identified ten young women from the local area who might possibly be their victim.

"Apart from one, no one has been in touch about any of them to check on progress. So, for all we know, these missing women might be back home. I'll check them out anyway," she said. "There are six from Ryebridge and the other four are from Ashton."

"Right age?" Harry asked.

"Right age-*ish*. I'll speak to the families, see if they can help."

"We can split the list, do half now and the rest after we've been to the Reid," Harry suggested.

"Okay, but you're driving," she said. "I've got a headache. The early start this morning didn't suit me."

Harry smiled. "Not like you. Sounds to me like too much wine last night. That new boyfriend of yours still keeping you up nights, is he?"

Jess stuck her nose in the air. She was getting tired of the jibes from the pair of them. So she had a boyfriend, big deal. Harry and Col needed to butt out of her private life and get partners of their own. "You can lose the tone, Lennox. Kyle's okay. He's only been living up here two minutes, but already he's got a good job. He's well-mannered and I enjoy his company."

Harry sniffed. "That's me told. I've only got your best interests at heart, you know. The job is important to you and you'll go far. You don't want some bloke muscling in and spoiling it."

"Kyle has no intention of spoiling anything. He knows what the job means to me."

Time to let it drop. Harry turned to Col. "Get anything from the CCTV?"

"Not without some hefty software to enhance the footage. It was misty early this morning, so the images are too indistinct to be of any use."

Shame. They could do with something. "Visit the local antique shops, see if they've sold the clothes she was wearing to anyone recently. Hettie will send you some photos." Wishful thinking, Harry knew. Whoever acquired that clothing had gone to a lot of trouble and sourcing it locally wouldn't have been clever. Too much risk of the shopkeeper remembering him. "Come on then, Jess, let's go and speak to the first three on the list."

They were about to leave the office when Harry's mobile rang. It was Melanie.

"I've got good news. This morning's victim has the name 'Lori' in a heart shape tattooed on her right upper arm. Could be her name, or that of a close friend or relative, but it might help."

Harry had the list in his hand. He cast his eyes down the names. There she was, number four, Lori Lansing, missing these last three weeks.

"Thanks, Melanie, we have her on our list of potentials. We'll pay the family a visit and then see you later at the Reid."

This was good news. Chances were they'd found their victim.

"I do have more information for you," Melanie said. "Can I suggest that you call into the Reid first?"

"Okay, see you shortly."

Jess followed Harry back to his office. "Why do I know that name?"

"Means nothing to me," Harry said. He sat at his computer in order to check the missing person record on the system — who reported her missing and the other details they had.

Soon, Harry had chapter and verse about the Lansing case in front of him. "Lori wasn't just a misper, she was a kidnap victim," he told Jess. "Her husband paid over a cool half million but never got his wife back."

Jess gave a low whistle. "A helluva lot of money for nothing. That and losing his wife must have left him in bits."

"And some. He must have been going out of his mind with worry, and then to lose the lot, wife and money, it's enough to send a man off his head." Harry read through the screenful of notes. "The case was handled by Hewitt's team. Lansing blamed the police, said we handled it wrong and threatened to sue." He looked at Jess. "It's a pity he didn't, that would have given that idiot Hewitt something to think about."

Jess didn't want to get into a slanging match about their colleague, this was too important. She was aware that Hewitt was sloppy, cut corners, but they were on the case now. If anyone could find out what happened to their victim, Harry could.

"For the first few days Lansing was quiet," Harry continued, "probably in shock, but then he became a real nuisance. He was rarely away from the front desk. He even went to the papers, made threats, until eventually the super had a word and things calmed down." He looked at Jess. "Why don't I remember that?"

"We've been a tad busy ourselves," she said. "Or have you forgotten the case we've just sorted? Now I think about it, I do recall reading something in the local rag. They interviewed the husband and he wasn't exactly flattering. I can understand him being angry though. As far as he was concerned, Hewitt failed him."

"Fair enough. So, Lansing had a point. We both know Hewitt is a past master at doing the bare minimum and getting away with it."

"What could Lansing do though? His wife had disappeared. What we should be asking is, if the victim from this morning is her, then where has she been the last three weeks?" Jess said.

Harry shook his head. "Held prisoner in the cold, and half-starved. Or there could be another explanation. For now, we see what Melanie's got for us and then talk to Adam Lansing. Explain what's happened, ask for a photo and any other help he can give us. I don't want to drag him into the morgue unless we have to — our victim looked so emaciated and I wouldn't want him to see her with her face all bashed in like that."

Jess was peering over his shoulder. "It says there were letters demanding money, five of them in the first week she was gone. The poor bloke must have gone through hell."

"I presume the letters will be in the evidence room somewhere. I'll get Col to dig them out," Harry said.

"Who is this Adam Lansing anyway?" Jess asked. "Do we know anything about him?"

"It says here that he owns a chain of small supermarkets situated throughout Greater Manchester. He's well-off and has never been in trouble with the police."

"It also says he's fifty-four, the wife is half his age. There may be something there," she said, giving Harry a knowing look.

"What sort of something?"

"Perhaps she got fed up, fancied company her own age and got in with the wrong crowd."

"Let's not get carried away with theories for now. A word with Melanie, see what's she got and then we'll visit Lansing. At least we'll have some facts to face him with," he said.

CHAPTER THREE

The problem was, the facts were not that palatable.

"Her skull is broken in several places," Melanie began. "She was hit about the head repeatedly with something wooden, a baseball bat possibly. We found splinters of wood in the wounds. Hettie will try to match them to a particular type of bat."

Jess shuddered. "Poor girl, she must have suffered."

"No, Jess," Melanie said. "The attack was vicious and protracted, but they did it after she was dead. Her skull, the bones of her face and her teeth are all but destroyed. I'm not surprised that when they left her in the open for us to find, they put a mask on her." Melanie picked up the short report she'd prepared for them. "What actually killed her was loss of blood. She's had an operation. There are two cuts on her lower body, in the flank area. They've been crudely stitched and no healing has taken place. When I do the autopsy I'll know more. Tests are ongoing for drugs and alcohol."

"An operation?" Harry asked. "Can you hazard a guess as to what it was for?"

"I have several theories," Melanie said grimly. "But I'm not prepared to speculate."

"You mentioned drug tests. D'you think she was a user?" Jess asked.

"Possibly. That could be why she's so thin, but we'll wait and see what the tests show up."

"You're sure about the beating?" Harry asked. "It seems like a lot of trouble to go to if the victim is already dead."

"It could be that for whatever reason, the killer was trying to hide her identity," Melanie said.

Something to consider, but why go to the trouble? Harry wondered. What was it about Lori Lansing that made the killer want to keep her death a secret?

"There is something else. Before she was killed the poor woman suffered a badly broken left hand," Melanie said. "I can't check the fingers as they've mostly all gone." She made a face. "More on that when we've done the tests. There is extensive bruising, her wrist is broken and the bones haven't even tried to heal. It could be the result of trying to defend herself. Apart from that, I can find no other marks on the body."

Harry nodded. Melanie had done well to find out this much so fast.

"There is evidence of near starvation which must have been ongoing for a while, longer than she would have been held prisoner, and debilitating. Her body is nothing but skin and bone. The poor girl needed medical help. I'd suggest an eating disorder."

"We'll check that out," Harry said. He was still wondering why the killer would want to conceal his victim's identity. Was he keeping it from Lori's husband? Did he want Adam Lansing kept in the dark about what had happened to his wife for as long as possible? If so, for what purpose?

"Any idea when she died? We've been given three weeks as a possibility," Jess said.

"That is difficult to ascertain until I open her up," Melanie said. "But I'd say two to three weeks ago seems a good enough estimation."

"If she was taken three weeks ago, d'you think that was long enough for the mistreatment — I'm thinking of the emaciation — to have an effect?" Harry asked.

"As I've said, I suspect Lori had been having a serious problem with food for some time, some sort of eating disorder. I've had a quick look and her oesophagus shows signs of frequent vomiting. You should ask her husband and check with her GP."

"However, we can give you something." Dr Hettie Trent, the Reid's senior forensic scientist, came up and joined them. "On the inside of her right wrist is a round blue mark, the type you get stamped with at clubs. The one on our victim's arm is reasonably clear, it's for the Rainbow. It's dated the sixth of October. So, she was alive then."

"Saturday, three weeks ago." Harry nodded. "I've looked at the record on the database. The letters started to arrive on the Tuesday morning."

"The Rainbow is that place on Ryebridge High Street," Jess added.

"D'you know it?" Harry asked.

"Kyle took me once but it's a bit pricy. It used to be the old cinema. It's been completely refurbished, and is high-end and plush, but there was a funny atmosphere. There were too many security staff for my liking. They put a dampener on the evening."

Harry didn't know the place. Nightclubs weren't his thing, he preferred to prop up the bar in the local pub. He was surprised someone had invested so much money in opening one in a relatively small town like Ryebridge. He wouldn't have thought there was the trade.

"She was given an overdose, then beaten to a pulp after she was dead. Her body was kept for a while before being left in the park for anyone to trip over. Seems to me someone didn't like the poor woman," he said.

"Something else," Hettie began. "I suspect that the clothes she has on were laundered before she was dressed in them. There is the faint remnant of a stain on the front of the skirt. I'll try to find out what it is."

"And I'll do the full autopsy at two this afternoon," Melanie confirmed. "Hopefully that will throw some light on what actually happened to the poor girl."

"And by this afternoon I'll have more on the clothing," Hettie added. "All of it looks genuine enough — from the late-Victorian, early-Edwardian era, even down to the lace drawers. The wig, too, it's real hair. It's all top quality. The mask, on the other hand, is papier-mâché, crudely made and painted."

"So, someone went to a lot of trouble, but I can't for the life of me see the significance of that odd outfit," Harry said.

"Perhaps when you find the killer, he'll explain it to you," Melanie said.

"I haven't told you the interesting bit yet," Hettie continued. "Even without a close examination, I can tell you that she didn't die in those clothes, nor did she wear them for long before she was found. As I said, they'd been freshly laundered. If she'd been in them for any length of time I'd have expected them to have been soiled by the slight decomposition that occurred prior to her being put in cold storage."

"You're saying that someone dressed her like that immediately before dumping the body?" Harry said.

"Yes. For whatever reason that's exactly what happened," Hettie said.

Interesting, but how it helped was guesswork at this point. Harry turned to Jess. "First off we'd better deal with the husband."

"Adam Lansing has left his office and is expecting us at his home," Jess told him. "Col rang ahead and told him we're on our way. He didn't sound too pleased, apparently."

"I'm not surprised," Harry said. "We weren't much help when he needed us, were we, or rather Hewitt wasn't. His wife disappears and despite the kidnapper's letters, we log her as just another misper and do nothing."

Jess pulled a face. "Another case for Rodders to review." She was talking about Superintendent Roderick Croft. "No doubt Hewitt will have some excuse at the ready."

Harry shook his head. "Just glad it wasn't me."

"You would never have made such a hash of it," she said.

"For now we tell Lansing the bare minimum. We confirm nothing until we know for sure it's her. After everything he's been through, we can't put him through the horror of how she died."

The visit to the Reid Centre left Harry puzzled. Why had Lori Lansing had to die in the first place? Had she upset someone? Argued? If she had, it must have been some almighty row for her to end up like she did. And who did she have in her life who was capable of doing such a thing? There was also the question of why the killer had hung onto the body and what had changed to make him give it up.

CHAPTER FOUR

Adam Lansing lived on the outskirts of Ryebridge in what Jess referred to as the 'posh end' — the exclusive Ashurst estate.

"Houses go for a fortune around here. Just this road and the two leading off it. They're huge, in their own grounds, surrounded by woods and fields, very desirable. Kyle has an uncle who lives round here somewhere, Clive Radford. Apparently he's got a full-length pool and gym in his back garden. He's a surgeon and part owner of that fancy private hospital, the Radford, off Mottram Road. You know, the one that opened last year."

Harry was only half listening. None of this was relevant. He was curious about Lansing though, curious about what made him tick and what made an attractive young woman half his age want to marry him. Perhaps Jess had it sorted and it was simply the money.

Lansing opened the door and invited them in. He was in his mid-fifties and looked every day of it. Harry could see at once that these last few weeks had taken their toll.

"Have you found her?" he said immediately. "You're new, not the idiot I dealt with initially. Please tell me you've got something positive for me and you're not simply reviewing the case."

What to tell him? Lansing was worried, the man's drawn face showed a glimmer of hope. He wanted good news, every atom of his being craved it. There wasn't any.

"We have found a body," Harry said gently. "It might be your wife but at this point we can't be certain."

Lansing looked at Harry. "She's been gone three weeks. Was she trapped somewhere? Was she being held prisoner? I couldn't bear it if that was the case. Why didn't the bastard kidnapper contact me again? He had the money he'd asked for and I'd have gladly given him more."

"We've no idea what happened, Mr Lansing. But we're investigating. It would help us if you could go over again the events of the day when your wife went missing."

Lansing shook his head wearily. "Again? You must have everything you need in your records. I've made a big enough nuisance of myself over the last couple of weeks. I can't imagine there's anyone in your nick who doesn't know the sorry tale by now."

"Please, indulge me, just one more time," Harry said.

Lansing threw his arms in the air in a gesture of resignation. "It was a bad day for early October, raining and unseasonably cold. I wanted Lori to stay at home — she wasn't feeling well, a bit of a hangover, I think, but she wouldn't listen. She reckoned she had to meet a mate for lunch regardless." His face fell. "I was a bit hard on her that morning. We argued and I said some things. I wanted her in the warm, out of the weather, but she wouldn't listen. In the end I gave in, made her some breakfast, sat and watched her eat it, and then waved her off. That was the last I saw of her."

"You watched her eat, you said. Was that because Lori had an eating disorder?" Jess asked.

"Yes, she did. She was always going on about how much she hated her body, how fat she was. We'd been to see the GP and he'd diagnosed her condition. Sometimes she was okay, but recently it'd started to get the better of her again. She was gorgeous just the way she was, but nothing I said would convince her. If I didn't sit and watch, she'd eat, go to the loo, stick her fingers down her throat and throw the lot up."

Jess nodded, although it wasn't something she understood. She loved her food.

"The day after Lori went missing, her car was found abandoned in the multi-storey in Ryebridge shopping centre," Lansing continued, "but there was no sign of her. Your forensic lot went over the car but found nothing. The police weren't particularly sympathetic. That first day they suggested she'd gone away, she was staying with a friend to spite me for the row we'd had. One bright spark even put forward the theory that she could have another man on the go." He sighed. "My Lori was a lot younger than me. I know what folk thought, but she loved me and we were happy."

"When did the first letter arrive?" Jess asked.

"She didn't come home that Saturday. I didn't know what to think. I tried all her friends but none of them had seen her — well, that's what they told me. The first letter came on the Tuesday morning and one each day after that. I was told the final letter would be instructions — where to leave the money and when. That's when I got scared. I started to question my decision not to have involved the police when that first letter arrived. It was a lot of money they wanted and I was taking a risk trusting the kidnapper to keep his word."

"You did change your mind," Harry said, "but made the mistake of leaving it until the last minute to call for help."

"I realised what a fool I'd been. In the beginning you lot were helpful. That DI Hewitt seemed to know what he was doing and I thought he was okay. Someone from his team stayed here at the house while we waited for the kidnapper to contact me. I'd got the money together and was prepared to hand it over. When I knew where and when, Hewitt's team would be waiting to pick him up." Lansing stuck his hands in his trouser pockets and turned to look out of the French windows. "I got a phone call, number withheld." He frowned. "I was to leave the money in a gym holdall in a specific place in the woods that border Ryebridge Park. I had the money ready, all half a million, but Hewitt said I should hold onto it. They took the bag, filled it with newsprint and went to do the drop, ready to nab him. The kidnapper didn't show. I was a nervous wreck. I waited for Hewitt to ring me, for word about Lori, but I heard nothing. Two hours after the time scheduled for the drop, I got another phone call from the kidnapper. He'd seen the police in the woods. He told me the deal was off. I pleaded with him, told him the money was waiting at my home. He said there'd be a dark blue van at the end of the drive in ten minutes. I was to put the holdall in the back and Lori would be free within half an hour." Lansing wiped away a tear. "By that time, I was alone and I decided not to involve the police again. What else could I do? I was desperate to get Lori back and had no choice but to do as instructed."

"Did you tell Hewitt?"

"Not straight away. Like I said, your lot had left me alone by then. The van pulled up and I put the money in the back. I knew I was taking a risk. I'd no guarantee the kidnapper would keep his word. I gave it a full hour and heard nothing. Then I rang Hewitt."

Harry felt sorry for the man. He'd parted with a small fortune, expected to get his wife back, only to have his life torn apart, losing both.

"I never heard from the kidnapper again. I blamed you lot — well, Hewitt anyway. His people had been seen. The kidnapper knew I hadn't kept my part of the deal, and not getting Lori back was my punishment."

Harry nodded. That was feasible, but it was just as likely that all along the kidnapper never intended to give her back. "Thanks for that," he said. "I'm sorry for making you go over it again. We can't second-guess what happened, we need the facts, and you're the best person to get them from."

"I've been a fool. He wanted my money and Lori was simply a pawn in his horrific game." At that, Lansing broke down. "Poor Lori. Can I see her?"

"It might be better to remember her as she was," Jess said gently.

"If I don't identify her, how will you know for sure that it's Lori?"

"We can do a DNA test for one," Harry told him. "I'll send an officer round to collect something of hers, perhaps you'd sort out a toothbrush or comb."

"Did she have any distinguishing marks?" Jess asked.

"She had her name tattooed inside a heart on her upper arm. It was neatly done."

That matched what they knew.

"There will be dental records too. I'll give you the name and address of her dentist," Lansing said.

Jess nodded, she hadn't the heart to tell him that, given the state of her face, dental records would be useless.

Harry got down to business. "I'd like to speak to Lori's friends. D'you have their contact details?"

"I've spoken to them all several times recently. They say they don't know anything, but then I'm not the police. You already have a complete list, it must be in your records somewhere. Hewitt wasn't interested in investigating too thoroughly. He was convinced Lori had done a runner, and that the demand for money was down to her and some new fancy man."

"But you were sent photos," Jess reminded him.

"Yes. Lori bound and gagged with someone's hands around her throat. You lot have them. I handed everything over at the time."

"D'you have a photo of Lori we could take away with us?" Harry asked. "You'll get it back."

Lansing went over to some shelves and removed one from its frame. It showed a young, attractive, dark-haired woman sitting at the wheel of an open-topped sports car. "Her twenty-first birthday present," he said, and smiled.

"Was Lori in the habit of colouring her hair?" Jess asked.

Lansing nodded. "All colours she had it, streaked, some of them vivid pink and green. I hated it but what d'you do? Lori was young and followed whatever trend was current."

"Give me a day or two and then we'll return with an update on the investigation so far," Harry said.

Lansing nodded. Harry noted the tears still in his eyes. The poor man was in bits. Their visit today had put all the ugly details back into sharp focus.

CHAPTER FIVE

"He seemed pretty genuine to me," Jess said, on their way back to the car.

Harry nodded. "His behaviour throughout would suggest that. I'll have a word with Hewitt once we're back at the nick. I'd like his take on things — if he can remember that far back."

"I don't like Hewitt much, do you?" she said.

"He's a lazy, incompetent sod. How he made inspector is a mystery to me."

Jess climbed into the car. "I often think the same about you, Lennox, but then you'll surprise me with some brilliant brainwave of a theory and everything falls into place."

Harry gave her a beaming smile. "So you think I'm brilliant. I can live with that, Jessie Wilde."

"Don't get carried away. They're merely flashes of brilliance, and infrequent at that."

Harry ignored the dig. "I'll deal with Hewitt. You print out that list of friends off the database. We'll have to make a start on them. What we need is inside knowledge, the stuff on Lori's life her husband didn't know about."

"You think there was something?" she asked.

Harry nodded. Too true he did. Lori Lansing had been a good-looking young woman, way out of her husband's league. What he had going for him was money, but he doubted that was enough to sustain her interest. "I'll lay odds there was another man in her life."

"Why would she risk everything for a bit on the side? She had a great life as it was," Jessie said.

"She was considerably younger than him for a start, and probably liked to go out nights with people her own age. We'll look at that list, ask around, and then you'll see what I'm getting at."

"I thought Adam Lansing a pleasant enough man. She married him, remember, so there must have been something between them," she said.

Harry gave her a funny look. "That something could well have been his money."

"Cynical as ever."

Harry wasn't sure what, but something about this case was niggling him. He couldn't put his finger on it but it just didn't fit together, that was for sure.

* * *

Back at the station, the first thing he did was seek out DI Bill Hewitt. He found him in his team's main office, standing deep in thought in front of the incident board.

"I hear she's turned up," he said, with a smile on his face. "I was convinced she'd planned the scam herself. I would have bet good money on her doing a runner with all that dosh. Seems I was wrong."

"You didn't think her disappearance suspicious?" Harry asked.

"I wasn't sure, but the husband was so positive that their marriage was good and that she'd never leave him. I felt sorry for the daft sod but in the end the money disappeared and there was no body. Hence my theory seemed sound." Hewitt shrugged.

"Well, her body has turned up now and Rodders has given the case to me."

Hewitt didn't seem bothered. "I'm up to me ears in it anyway, mate." An easy excuse that irritated Harry. "Couldn't take it on even if I wanted to. You've got access to the records though, statements and the like. Fill your boots."

"Did you speak to Lori's friends?" Harry asked.

"Only her best mate as I recall. Not much help, holding back, I thought. Tight-lipped bitch that worked in some bar. If Lori Lansing was planning anything, she'd know about it, I'd stake my pension on that."

"Name?"

"Debra Dobson. Her details are on the system, she gave a statement."

Harry left him to it and returned to his own office. This Debra, whoever she was, needed finding. They had to see what she could tell them about what was happening back then. He checked the time. If they were attending the autopsy, they should get a move on. "Jess, we've a date at the morgue."

"I've printed out that list of Lori's mates. There are quite a few, they'll take some getting through."

"She was closest to one called Debra, according to Hewitt. We'll start with her."

"He does remember the case then."

"Yes, but he doesn't see it as one of his great failures. He reckons he believed she'd done a runner with money her husband paid over. Well, he got that all wrong," Harry said.

"Easy way out as usual with Hewitt."

Jess was right on that score. He checked the time again, they should make tracks. The trail for this case was already cold, and they desperately needed all the help the forensic team could give them. Hettie Trent and her boss, Prof Hector Steele, were the best there were in his estimation. Hopefully, with that pair on the case they'd get somewhere.

"Col," he called to the young DC. "While we're gone, have a look at the local antique shops and see if any of them have sold any sort of Victorian clothing recently. She was wearing the full outfit, including wig, so it might have come from more than one shop."

"I'd like to know why he dressed her like that in the first place," Jess said. "Men's minds, there's just no working them out."

"Are you doing anything tonight?"

Harry had asked the question so matter of factly that it threw Jess for a moment, and she grappled for a response. "You asking me out?"

"Yes." He grinned at the surprised look on her face. "I thought you and me could give the Rainbow a whirl."

Now she understood. "I'll have to sort it with Kyle."

"Jealous type, is he?"

"No, but I don't want any confusion."

"No confusion, Wilde, just good old-fashioned work."

CHAPTER SIX

Harry and Jess watched the proceedings from the gallery, standing a few metres above the table where Melanie was working. By the time they arrived, she had Lori Lansing prepped and ready for the first incision. She raised her eyes and nodded to the pair, the scalpel in her hand.

This bit always made Harry feel sick. He took a deep breath and averted his eyes.

"I can confirm that she was savagely beaten about the head and face — post-mortem thankfully. She was kept somewhere, perhaps in the open or a shed, prior to being put in a cold store or fridge," Melanie said. "I can't say how long she was kept for, I'm afraid, but you have other clues, thanks to Hettie. All I can say is that by the time she was put in cold storage, decomposition had already begun. The date stamp on her wrist says six October. Looking at the decomposition, I'd say she was kept in the open for several days before being chilled."

Killed, kept somewhere, and when the killer realised he was in for the long haul, he'd stashed her somewhere cold. Harry shuddered. He wondered why he hadn't simply let her be found earlier.

"The fingers on both hands have been removed and not neatly. At a guess I'd say a garden tool like secateurs was used." They watched Melanie examine the stumps through her magnifying glass. "Take a swab," she instructed the technician. "There is what looks like soil here. It might give us something. Her eyes have gone and the facial tissue is very bloated." She looked up at the pair. "I doubt her nearest and dearest would recognise her now. Can I suggest that you find some other way to confirm her identity? It would be too distressing for a loved one to see her like this. We can do it by DNA instead."

Whoever had killed Lori had gone to a great deal of trouble to ensure there was no simple way of identifying her. What he couldn't understand was why, and why leave the tattoo? "If you take a photo of the tattoo on her arm I'll show it to the husband," Harry said. "He's already described it but I'd prefer to be sure."

"I'm surprised the killer left it intact," Melanie said, echoing his thoughts. "It's distinctive and easily recognisable to those who knew her well. Given he went to such lengths to conceal her identity, it's a bit of a mystery.

"Prior to death, two incisions were made on either side of her abdomen, the flank areas." Melanie cut the stitches and opened up both wounds. She looked up at the pair. "Both her kidneys are missing. I'd say the operation was carried out by a surgeon. Once the kidneys had been harvested, both renal arteries were cut in two. The incisions look purposeful, not accidental. Whoever operated on this woman definitely did not intend her to survive the surgery."

Jess looked at Harry and whispered, "She wouldn't have lived anyway without her kidneys. But why? Why take them?"

"There is a ready market out there for spare body parts, Jess," he breathed. "Not that I'm aware of organ theft being a problem in Ryebridge."

Melanie continued her careful, thorough examination. She looked closely at each organ in turn and stopped when she'd emptied the stomach contents. "Her last meal was a bacon sandwich and coffee," she called up to them. "Sounds like breakfast to me."

The mention of a bacon sandwich made Harry think of something. "Will you give me a moment? I just want a quick word with Lansing."

He went out into the corridor and rang him. Lansing was in a meeting and urged him to be quick. "I miss my wife but I've still got to keep the business afloat."

"On the morning she disappeared, you told us you made Lori some breakfast. Can you recall exactly what you gave her?"

"Odd question. Why is that important now?"

"Please, indulge me, what did she have to eat?" Harry said.

"As it happens, I do remember. Food and Lori were often at odds so it was a pleasant change to cook for her. If she ate anything at breakfast, the most I could hope for was a little cereal, but that morning she asked me to make her a bacon sandwich. We had a conversation about it, she said she fancied one and that was that. She ate the lot and drank a mug of strong coffee to wash it down."

Harry's hunch had been right, another tick in the box for this being Lori. "Thank you, Mr Lansing, we should have some answers for you soon."

Harry returned to the gallery. "Sorry about that, but I recalled something her husband said when we spoke. The stomach contents, bacon and coffee, that's what Lori had for breakfast on the day she disappeared. Adam Lansing has every moment of that last day imprinted on his brain and clearly recalls making it for her."

Melanie looked thoughtful. "She must have died within a few hours of eating it then, it's only partly digested."

Harry nudged Jess. "Confirmation, if we needed it, that she has been dead these last three weeks and not held captive somewhere. The fact she's thin has to be down to her condition, which in some ways is a relief. I'd like to know where the killer kept the body prior to leaving it in the open. He must have access to a pretty big fridge."

"Now this is interesting," Melanie said, looking up at them again. "Lori was pregnant, about eight weeks."

They hadn't anticipated that.

"Perhaps that's why she fancied the bacon sandwich," Jess said.

"I wonder if Lansing knew," Harry whispered.

"Any reason he wouldn't?" Jess asked. "She would be at that doing-a-test stage."

"He's never mentioned it," Harry said, "and I'm sure he would have at some point."

"I'll do a DNA test on the foetus," Melanie said. "If the husband isn't the father, you need to know. Ask him to pop in and we'll take a saliva swab."

"If he isn't the father, then who is?" Jess asked. "We've no other likely candidates."

"Not yet," Harry said. The notion that there may have been another man in Lori's life hadn't occurred to him but it should have done.

"That list of friends, we need to speak to each and every one of them," Jess said. "If there was another man in her life, we need to know who he was. Debra Dobson is the one to ask. Her and Lori were close. If she was going to confide in anyone, it would be her."

Jess was right. He sent a quick text to Col back at the station, asking him to find out where she worked.

"As if the operation wasn't enough, as a final act Lori was injected with heroin," Melanie told them. "The injection site is on her upper arm. She would have known nothing, just rolled over and died. As I said, the beating came later." Melanie looked at the pair. "The body isn't pleasant to look at but it doesn't reflect how she was killed. All the injuries, apart from the surgery, were inflicted after death."

Jess was having trouble getting her head round it all. Why beat a dead body so badly? What purpose did it serve? "D'you think someone didn't want us to find out who she was?" she whispered to Harry.

"That tattoo on her arm is distinctive, so fat chance of that. But we'll keep it in mind."

Harry's mobile beeped, it was a reply from Col. With a sigh he passed the phone to Jess. "Guess where Debra works."

"The Rainbow. Well, there's a coincidence. I wonder if Lori went there to meet her."

"We'll find out later," Harry said. "Who owns the club?"

"I've no idea, but the manager is a man called David Parsons. I know him from school. He's okay. From what I saw when I was there with Kyle, he seems to know his job and as I said, he certainly makes sure the place is kept trouble free."

"It has an odd atmosphere is what you said."

"I thought all those bouncers made for security overload," Jess said. "It got a bit oppressive seeing those suited thug types standing at every door, but it does ensure there's no trouble. You know what Ryebridge people can get like with a drink inside them."

"I'll pick you up at eight," Harry said. "I trust we can get a meal there."

"We can, but the food isn't cheap."

"Expenses, Jess, we'll be working, remember."

CHAPTER SEVEN

The plush, upmarket nightclub called the Rainbow, formerly the old Ryebridge cinema, had been completely refurbished. Once through the main doors the sight of the bouncers in every doorway brought on that familiar uneasy feeling in the pit of Jess's stomach. Harry didn't feel so happy either. He didn't do posh, but tonight he'd made a supreme effort and was obviously uncomfortable. He straightened his tie and nudged Jess as they walked into the bar. "Smart place. Glad I wore my best suit, they might have thrown me out otherwise. You don't look too shabby yourself, by the way."

Jess was wearing a sexy black dress, clingy and short, totally unlike her usual working apparel of casual trousers and a shirt. "We certainly don't look like old bill, and with those security blokes eyeing all the customers, I'd say that was a bonus. They've not got a smile between them."

"Whether they cotton on or not doesn't matter. They're not going to create a scene, wouldn't look good in front of the other punters. For tonight, despite the atmosphere, I'd say we were quite safe. We do need that quiet word with Debra though, but we'll be careful. No need to upset anyone." Harry winked.

A waiter showed the pair to a table and handed Harry the drinks menu.

"I'll have a bottle of lager," he said.

"Mine's a white wine, please," Jess added.

Harry turned to watch the waiter go, while checking an image on his mobile. "That's Debra behind the bar. The blonde with all the makeup on her face."

"Want me to go and speak to her?" Jess asked. "No need to approach her mob-handed."

Harry nodded. "Be careful, mind. There's two of those goons by the bar. Don't say anything to spook them."

Jess turned to look at the heavily built men, both in suits and bow ties. "They're probably here just to reassure people that the place is safe. You can't say that about most drinking venues in Ryebridge. Well, here goes. Wish me luck." Jess got up from the table and made her way over to the bar, and Debra.

The young woman was putting glasses away. She looked at Jess and frowned. "The waiter will bring your drinks over, love."

Jess smiled encouragingly. "I wanted a quick word. Someone told me you're Lori's friend."

As soon as Jess uttered the name, Debra's face fell. She glanced nervously at the bouncers. "Whatever it is, I can't help. Lori disappeared and she's never been in touch, so that's us done."

"Lori is dead, Debra. She was murdered."

It took a few seconds for this to sink in. "I still can't talk to you," the young woman hissed, emphatic. "Leave me alone. If one of the security blokes sees me talking to you, he won't like it."

"There are some things we'd like to know about Lori, things I doubt even her husband is aware of."

"You're police, aren't you? You could get me sacked, or even killed," she whispered. "Him over there by the door." She nodded at another security bloke. "He finds out who you are and I'll get the push, as well as the rest."

"Was she having an affair, Debra?"

"How should I know?"

"You and her were close."

"Look, leave me alone. I can't tell you anything."

"But you do know something, I can tell by the look on your face. Lori was murdered in a horrific way, and we need your help. Would you prefer to tell us down at the station?"

Jess didn't want to frighten Debra but she wasn't getting anywhere, and they needed a break.

"She had someone but I've no idea who he was. She wouldn't talk about him, she was terrified that Adam would find out."

Debra was lying — she couldn't look Jess in the eye. She knew very well who Lori had been seeing.

Making sure the security guys didn't see her, Jess passed her a card. "You have to talk to us, Debra. We need information that only you can give us. I can meet you somewhere private, no one need know. What d'you say?"

"I'll think about it."

Jess went back to the table. "Debra might help but I get the impression she's afraid of someone — no, more than that, she's terrified."

That didn't surprise Harry. "I reckon we've been clocked. See that bloke at the table by the window? He didn't take his eyes off you while you were talking to Debra."

"That's David Parsons, the manager." Jess smiled and waved at him. "I told you earlier, I've known him since we were kids. We're new here, he's just keeping an eye, that's all."

"Is he an old boyfriend?"

"I went to school with him, but he was a year ahead of me. He was a bit of a swot, earmarked for greater things than a nightclub in Ryebridge, so something must have happened to spoil his plans."

"Why don't you ask him?" Harry suggested.

"That will just draw attention to us," Jess protested. "Next thing we'll have security asking questions."

"Go on, he'll think it odd if you ignore him." He grinned. "Try your luck, and see if he knew Lori while you're at it."

"Don't move a muscle while I'm gone. If the waiter wants to know about food, I'll have the sea bass."

* * *

Jess approached Parsons, wondering how he'd greet her. It'd been a while since school. In his last couple of years, Parsons had been the butt of numerous bullies, and some of them had been Jess's friends from her class. "I thought it was you but I couldn't be sure," she said. "What're you doing here?"

David Parsons indicated to the chair opposite his and Jess sat down. "I couldn't be sure it was you either." He smiled bashfully. "We've all changed so much, grown up and moved on."

"I won't intrude if you're waiting for someone."

"No, I work here," he explained, telling her what she already knew. "I'm the manager."

"Well done. D'you like the job?"

"It's not how I planned to spend my working life but it pays well and I get a free rein. It also allows me to stay in Ryebridge. I never had any ambitions to move away. You joined the police so I heard."

Jess cast her eyes around the room, they were being watched. Three of the security men had their eyes trained on them. "Yes, and I work locally too. But I'm off duty tonight, having a bite to eat with a colleague."

"I saw you talking to Debra before. Anything important? Are you currently embroiled in a case that involves the club?"

He'd asked the question casually enough but there was a look on his face that smacked of worry. She smiled. "Not really. We're investigating a murder and she was friendly with the victim, Lori Lansing," she explained. "It's probable that Lori came here. Did you know her by any chance?"

The sound of the name brought a scowl to his face. "Lots of people come here, Jess. I don't recognise the name. Was Debra helpful?"

"Not at all. She reckons there's nothing she can tell us." Jess said this in an effort to protect Debra.

David Parsons appeared to accept her explanation. He got to his feet. "Better get on, work to do." He smiled. "Nice talking to you, Jess. Take care of yourself."

Jess returned to her own table and sat down opposite Harry. "Nothing. And if you ask me, he was scared stiff."

"Those goons never took their eyes off you either." Harry looked around and shuddered. "Mind if we go? This place is giving me the creeps. If you're up for it, we can get fish and chips down the road."

CHAPTER EIGHT

Tuesday

"Harry!"

He was about to leave the house the next morning, when he heard someone calling his name. "Sorry, mate, I know it's short notice but I'll have to ask you to leave."

That was a blow, something Harry could do without. Col's mate, Ryan, had taken him in after he'd had the bust-up with Jess. Just over a week later, he'd obviously changed his mind. "Too messy, am I? Feel free to say what you think. It's done for me before."

Ryan laughed. "It's not that. I've got family coming to stay. My cousin is looking for a place to live for a few months while he's at uni, so I'm going to need your room." Ryan spread his arms wide. "I've no choice, really I haven't. You know what relatives are like."

Harry nodded as if he understood, but inside he was quietly seething. Perhaps Jess was right and he should sort something more permanent. "Do I have until the weekend?"

An apologetic look crossed Ryan's face. "Can we say no later than Friday?"

Harry nodded. What choice did he have? It had been good of Ryan to offer at the time and he was grateful, but Col had indicated that he could rent the room for as long as he needed. So much for that. Sometime this morning he'd have to scour the web and contact the local letting agents. A chore he wasn't looking forward to.

By the time he reached the station, Harry was in a foul mood. He didn't say much, just gathered the team together in the main office to give their feedback on what they'd got.

Jess began. "The staff at the Rainbow are a right tight-lipped bunch," Jess told them. "Neither Debra Dobson nor the manager will admit to knowing anything about Lori. Debra is definitely holding back, as we've been told the two were close. As for David Parsons, the manager, I'm not sure. If Lori had been to that club then he would have remembered her — she was a good-looking young woman. I know him from way back, and I got the impression he was afraid to speak."

"Why would that be?" Harry said to the group. "What kind of fear binds people together like that?"

"We know who the manager is but do we know who actually owns the club?" Jess asked. "They've got heavy-duty muscle watching every door in the place. Someone is paying them."

"I've had a go but trying to find out is like wading through treacle," Col said. "I've been on to Companies House, and all they'll say is that it's owned by 'Rainbow Enterprises', whoever they are. They in turn are owned by a company with an address in the Channel Islands that has at least a dozen other companies in the UK."

Harry addressed the two uniformed officers sitting at the front. "Are there any rumours on the streets? Anything at all about the pedigree of the club?"

Constable Jack Aldred, the younger of the pair, looked at his partner and then back at Harry, obviously unsure whether to say something or not. "There's never any trouble and that's unusual for Ryebridge. Most weekends there's a ruck at one watering hole or the other, but never the Rainbow. But it's not popular and that's odd. There's something wrong there, but I've no idea what."

The second officer, Bob Tait, cleared his throat. "I did hear a rumour a few months back . . ." He shook his head. "I don't know if there's anything in it but if there is, you won't like it. I know I found it hard to get my head round."

"Spit it out," Harry said.

The officer looked around at the expectant faces, then uttered the name. "Terry Blackwood."

The words hung in the air. No one said anything for several seconds, until, finally, Jess broke the silence.

"That's . . . that's not good, in fact it's the worst news of all. If you're right, it could give us a shed load of trouble."

Harry looked bemused. Since coming to work at Ryebridge station, he'd heard the name no more than a couple of times and always to do with crimes outside their area. "Come on then, someone tell me about the man. What makes him so scary?"

"Where to begin?" Jess said. "He's a villain, violent and old school. He's a crime boss who rules his people with an iron fist. We don't hear about him because he's clever — clever and ruthless. These last few years he's tended to take a back seat but mark my words there's nothing cracks off in Ryebridge and the surrounding area without Blackwood giving it his approval." She looked around at the others. "If he's active again, then we've got a problem, and we need to ask why he's operating again. He'll be using the Rainbow as a cover for something, and that could be at the bottom of why Lori was killed. The problem with Blackwood is that no one has managed to get any evidence against the man that sticks. Every case that's been put before the CPS has been thrown out."

Harry paced the room. He didn't like the sound of this. He was used to organised crime, there'd been plenty of big-time villains in Glasgow, but so far the villains and killers he'd encountered in Ryebridge had worked alone, not had a gang of thugs watching their backs.

"Where do we find him?" he asked after a while.

This took Jess aback. "You want us to speak to him? Don't you think it's a little early in the case to give ourselves the aggro? We've nothing on him, and we certainly don't want to go storming round to his place without good reason."

"He owns that club, we know Lori went there and his staff won't or can't talk to us. Why shouldn't we have a word?"

"Can I suggest we first find something concrete to tackle Blackwood with," Jess said. "A vague complaint that his staff are being careful about what they tell us won't cut it. We'd be wise not to antagonise the man until we have to. My instincts tell me that something's going on, but we need more information before we barge in."

While Jess was giving Harry the benefit of her advice, Colin had answered her mobile, which was lying on her desk.

"That information we need might be about to come our way," he said with a smile. "That was Debra Dobson. She wants to meet up with you — just you, mind, on your own. Twelve thirty at the bus station café."

Jess gave him a big smile. "I knew it. Lori was her best friend and she has to talk to someone." She turned to Harry. "If she spills her guts about Blackwood or any of them at the club, that's our way in, but we'll have to offer her police protection."

"Get what we want and she can have all the protection she needs." Harry felt better — a lead at last. "Get anything on the clothing?" he asked Col.

"I got nothing from the local antique shops. Don't deal in it, apparently. But one of the shopkeepers told me that there's a weekly antique fair out Cheshire way at this time of year, and several of the regular sellers specialise in vintage and antique clothing. It's on tomorrow, so I thought I'd take a look."

Harry nodded. A good place to buy, a lot of people milling about, and unlike with a local shop, the sellers weren't likely to remember an individual customer. Nevertheless, they'd have to try.

"In that case, Col, take Bob with you and see what you can turn up."

CHAPTER NINE

Meeting over, Jess followed Harry into his small office. "Why the face, Lennox? What've you got to look so grim about? We'll get a handle on the case once Debra talks to me. If it does have anything to do with Blackwood, we'll bring him in."

"It's not work," he said. "Ryan's chucking me out. I've got to get somewhere else to live by Friday or I'm on the street."

"That is short notice," Jess said. "What've you done to upset him?"

"Nothing. I did ask if I was too untidy but he didn't look as if he'd noticed. He said he hadn't anyway."

"Oh, he'll have noticed, you live like a slob." She folded her arms. "There's only one thing for it then. Get yourself a short-term lease and look at buying something. You can't continue like this."

But Harry wasn't listening. "I can't think what's happened to make him change his mind about me, but it has nothing to do with being neat and tidy. He made some lame excuse about family staying and a relative needing the room for uni but he has seven bedrooms, Jess. How much room does he need?"

She wasn't going to win this one, not yet anyway. "Okay, I'll leave you to it and while you sort your domestic crisis, I'll see what we know about Lori's other friends."

Jess returned to the main office and sat down at her computer. She ploughed through the list of names and their occupations, but none of them jumped out at her. They all had fairly ordinary jobs, some were married, some not, but all appeared to be law-abiding.

She gazed at the photo of the young woman with the dark spiky hair. "Who did you upset, Lori? And why did you marry Adam? Was the big attraction his money, or was there something else?"

"Talking to yourself, eh? You know what that's a sign of." Col grinned at her and nodded towards Harry's office. "What's wrong with him this morning?"

"Your friend Ryan has asked him to move out."

Col pulled a face. "I'm surprised. That house of his is huge, and I know he needs the money."

"Family stuff, he told Harry, but don't you get involved. He needs to sort himself a place of his own anyway."

Jess continued to scan through the names, though she had already convinced herself it was a waste of time. If anyone knew about Lori's secrets, it would be Debra. "Where does Blackwood live?" she asked Col.

"I'm told he has a place in Saddleworth," he replied. "It'll be some huge house with loads of land and views of the hills."

"Big house for one bloke."

"He does have a wife and two sons," Col said. "The lovely Carla, and two boys at boarding school somewhere."

"He does have connections with Ryebridge too," one of the uniforms added. "He was brought up here and his mother still lives up near the hospital. He often stays with her when he's at the club. He's also a member of Ryebridge's exclusive golf club."

"He'll know people in that case. He's a wealthy man, probably has influence. I wonder if he knew Lansing and Lori socially."

"I should imagine so. Lansing is a member of the golf club too," the uniform said.

"You sure about that?"

"Yes. The club donated to the Police Benevolent Fund last year, and I recall seeing the pair at the cheque presentation."

Jess got up from her desk and went to find Harry. It wasn't much, but given Lori went to Blackwood's club, she couldn't ignore the connection. Important or not, Harry should know about this, and then they'd decide whether or not to speak to Lansing again.

* * *

"Bloody estate agents. Everything they've got on their books costs a fortune in rent and they all want a hefty deposit."

Jess sighed and pointed to an ad on his screen. "Look. New builds near me, reasonably priced and handy for work. Why not go and take a look? The show house is open for viewing and they'll all be ready within the month."

Not what Harry wanted, but he was beginning to think he had little choice. Renting would cost him a fortune but he had to do something.

"We could go and take a look together," she suggested. "Make the right decision and you can move back in with me until you complete on the deal."

Harry beamed at her. "We'll grab a sandwich from the canteen and go and have a look later."

"Also, I've discovered that Terry Blackwood is often in Ryebridge, and both he and Lansing belong to the same golf club. They are of an age, and I'm wondering if they know each other."

"We could always go and ask Lansing. Ask Col to contact him, let him know we're on our way."

Jess nodded. "We could swing by those houses on the way back. We look at the showhouse and then I'll keep my date with Debra."

Harry nodded. He might as well go with the plan. Kind of her as it was, Jess wouldn't put up with him for long, and living on the streets wasn't a pleasant option.

* * *

Lansing invited them in and led them through to the spacious living room. "You've got some information for me?"

"Not about Lori, but we wondered if you know a man called Terry Blackwood."

At the mention of the name, Lansing immediately became nervous. "I know him from way back. Once upon a time, we were neighbours, our parents lived on the same terrace. Not that we mixed much. Terry was always a troublemaker, in and out of borstal." He looked enquiringly at the pair. "But you must already know about him, surely. Given his reputation, he's bound to be well known in police circles."

"He gives the impression of being a different man these days," Jess said.

"He tries hard at being a pillar of the community, but no one's taken in by his antics."

"Could Lori have known him?"

Lansing shrugged. "I doubt it."

"I ask because Lori did frequent Blackwood's club, the Rainbow."

"Lori went there to mix with her own age group, not old fogies like Blackwood." Lansing turned away from them. "I hated it when Lori went there, but she liked the place. I didn't approve, but what could I do? I have no interest in going to clubs but I didn't think it fair to stop her if she wanted to go."

Jess nodded. She felt sorry for the man. The age difference between the pair had obviously started to grate away at the marriage.

"Thanks, Mr Lansing. We'll keep you posted with our findings."

CHAPTER TEN

"They're built out of fake stone and they look like little boxes. I can't live in one of them."

They'd stopped to take a quick look at the new houses Jess thought would suit him. "Well, I live in one, and given your situation you can't afford to be choosy."

"You've done things to your house, the garden and stuff. You've put up hanging baskets, re-done the outside paint-work. You've given your house the stamp of individuality."

"You can do the same."

"I won't though. I'll never find the time and like you're always telling me, I'm a born slob."

"Alright, Lennox, if not one of these, what? I won't see you on the streets but I won't put up with you for longer than a few weeks either."

No mincing words there, blunt as ever, and Jess meant it. "You can drop me at the station and then you take another look at that website and get some alternative viewings organised."

He took on a faraway look. "Where I lived in Dunoon it was lovely. The house was on a hill, built of real stone and it overlooked the sea."

"It was a family house and Dunoon is very different from Ryebridge," she pointed out. "No sea for starters."

"Now you're making fun and it's not fair. Look, give me a couple of days and I promise I'll find something."

Jess hoped so. Harry's domestic arrangements were beginning to get on her nerves. She'd never known any of her colleagues have so much difficulty finding somewhere to live.

They pulled into the station car park, Jess hopped out of the car and made for her own. "I'll see you later. Let's hope my little chat with Debra bears fruit. We certainly need something."

* * *

The café at Ryebridge bus station was old and over the years had fallen into disrepair. The windows, draped in discoloured net curtains, let in a draught. The tables were Formica-topped and chipped, the chairs a bright orange plastic. Jess cast her eyes over the food on offer and decided not to bother. Debra Dobson was waiting for her in the far corner and, despite numerous notices forbidding it, was smoking.

"Bert don't mind." She nodded at the man behind the counter. "He's a heavy smoker himself. Besides, there's no one else in here. Place is falling apart and folk don't use it much."

Sitting opposite Debra, Jess wondered why the glamorous Lori had been so close to this woman. She struggled to come up with something they might have had in common. They were very different for a start. Debra was older and the extra years hadn't been kind. She could only be in her mid-thirties but her face was already lined, and she had that gaunt look around her cheeks. Jess wondered if she was a drug taker. Perhaps that's what they'd had in common.

"You mustn't come to the club again," Debra said firmly. "Terry clocks you and I'm done for. He can spot police a mile off and I don't fancy a beating."

"Lori's been murdered. I'm part of the team investigating. She visited the club and I'm curious to know why. I need answers or I'm afraid I will have to go back there, and this time it'll be official."

"Look, you should back off. Getting involved with Terry Blackwood is dangerous, even for the police. He finds out that I spoke to you and he'll kill me, you too if he considers you a danger to his scams." She glanced nervously out of the window. "And it's not just Terry anymore. He's brokering some deal with a villain from out of town."

"D'you have a name for this guy?"

"No names, love, it's more than my life's worth."

"You said that Terry is a villain, that's a serious accusation," Jess said. "I don't want to put either of us in danger, Debra. All I want to know is why Lori went to the club."

"Terry invited her. We were out shopping one afternoon, and we bumped into him. He took to Lori straight away, and I think she was flattered by the attention. He likes to have pretty young women around him and she fitted the bill perfectly. It was risky though." Debra gave a sly smile. "You won't have met his wife, Carla. She's stood by Terry through thick and thin, but she's a jealous bitch. Terry believes he owes her. He knows full well that if she ever found out about his womanising she'd have his guts. Not that she's overly fond of her husband but she doesn't like being made a fool of. Carla knows plenty and could really drop him in it." She looked at Jess. "Where Carla's concerned, Terry knows it's in his interests to play the game."

"D'you think she found out about Lori?"

"What you're asking is could Carla have killed her." Debra grinned. "Jealous, yes, but killer? No way. Besides, Carla knew Lori. Lori was an occasional member of the theatre group she runs in Ryebridge. Carla's very protective of her little group and likes to take care of them."

"I've seen the adverts for the plays they put on." Jess smiled. "So, you doubt Carla would be jealous enough to do Lori harm?"

"She wouldn't, but Terry is another matter. If Lori crossed him, if things got awkward and she became a nuisance, he might."

"Was Terry fond of Lori?"

"I doubt he's capable of being fond of anyone," Debra said. "Lori was just another pretty girl to show off around the club. Terry has no morals. He knows her husband, they've played golf together, but that didn't stop him. Within days of meeting, they were seeing each other. Anyone asks, you didn't get that from me. By the time Lori disappeared it'd been going on for several weeks. I told you, Terry is that type of man. Always has to have someone young and pretty in his life. The moment he set eyes on Lori, her fate was sealed."

"Lori was killed and her body kept somewhere for a while." Jess said nothing about the beating. "Is he capable of that?"

"He's capable of anything. Terry has a temper, he lashes out and then gets one of his goons to tidy up. But I don't recall any argument or Terry saying anything bad about Lori. When she hadn't been in for a couple of weeks, he asked about her. He asked me if I knew what had happened to her. He thought her husband had got suspicious and sorted her out."

Jess made a mental note of that one. "How does Blackwood earn his money? The club is busy but it wouldn't support that big house of his and the lifestyle."

Debra shrugged. "He's a crook, love. And the Rainbow isn't his only club. He's got another dozen across Greater Manchester. He deals in drugs and girls and he has a lucrative loan business. He's got most of Ryebridge by the throat, and those who've had dealings with him haven't always walked away happy, if you get my meaning. Blackwood has caused a lot of anger in the town. For the last two years he's terrorised folk right, left and centre. Blackwood isn't a popular man." She took a long drag on her cigarette. "But the day will come, you just watch. Mark my words, one of these days Terry will take on the wrong person, and that might happen sooner than he thinks." She let out a throaty cough. "Bloody chest, it'll be the death of me."

"Thanks, Debra, what you've told me is very useful."

"There is something else," Debra said, catching her breath. "I've no idea what it's all about but there've been a lot of odd phone calls to the club recently. Most of them are from some foreign doctor at that private hospital on Mottram Road. Blackwood might be into something new, or he might be ill. I've had my ear to the ground for a while but no joy."

That got Jess's attention. She made a mental note to try and find out. She'd see if any of the team knew anything about it when she got back. If she got the chance, she'd also ask Kyle. "You sure Blackwood's not into something much simpler, like drugs?"

Debra shook her head. "He's already into that, but don't quote me. No, this is something else."

"Who does he mix with, apart from his golfing mates and people from the clubs?"

"That's about it really." Debra thought for a moment. "If you do find out that he's ill, promise you'll tell me?"

Debra's sudden frankness surprised Jess. "When did you last see Lori?"

"A few weeks back, at the start of this month. There was a do at the club. She came in and spoke to Terry. I heard them making arrangements to meet later that night, some party at one of Terry's friends. Lori wasn't sure if she should go, she was afraid that Carla or her own husband would find out. She said more and more people had got to know about the affair, and that it was only a matter of time." She pulled heavily on her cigarette and blew a plume of stale tobacco into the air. "In the end I think fear got the better of her, because I don't reckon she turned up for that party. Terry was in a foul mood the next day." She smiled. "She must have stood him up — brave girl. Terry wouldn't like that. I tried ringing her to find out what was going on, but that husband of hers said she was visiting family. I didn't believe him. I decided that he must have found out about Terry and there'd been a right ruck. I half expected her to come back to the club with a black eye, but she didn't. She didn't come back. I never saw Lori again."

CHAPTER ELEVEN

Harry lifted his head from the computer screen and nodded at Col, who was hovering by his desk. "Important?"

"Could be. Melanie rang, she says your mobile's turned off and she wants to speak to you urgently."

Harry picked up his phone — the battery was dead. "Stick it on charge, will you?" He went into the main office and called Melanie from the phone on Jess's desk. This might be just the piece of the puzzle they were short of.

"I no longer need a DNA sample from Adam Lansing," she began.

Good or bad news? Harry couldn't tell from her tone. "Oh? In that case, how do we find out who the father is?"

"Find me a likely suspect willing to give a DNA sample and I'll tell you."

"How d'you know it's not Lansing's baby?"

"I requested Lori's medical records," Melanie said. "She wanted a child, but her and Lansing were having difficulties. They decided on a sperm donor and a suitable candidate was being sought through the Maternity department at Ryebridge. Their doctor confirmed that her husband was infertile."

"Could the infant be a product of that procedure?"

"No. She hadn't begun the programme, and — here's the interesting bit — she rang the clinic a week before she disappeared to cancel."

"Because she knew she was already pregnant."

"I would suggest so," Melanie said.

Harry finished the call and rang Jess, wondering what to make of the news. Lori must have had a lover, but who was he?

"I'm on my way back with news," she told him before he got a word in. "And it's big."

"I've got big news too. I'm gathering the team together for a briefing. See you shortly."

* * *

Adam Lansing was not the father of Lori's baby. That'd give the team plenty to think about, but more importantly, it might have given Lansing a motive for killing his wife.

"I don't see it," Col said when he'd heard Harry's theory. "If he was hiding her body, why the song and dance for those two weeks? Surely he'd want things to quieten down, the attention to be anywhere but on him."

Harry was just about to respond when Jess arrived. She threw her jacket on the back of her chair and sat down. "I've just come from speaking to Debra Dobson. Remember her? She's the barmaid at the Rainbow. She told me that Lori was having an affair."

This wasn't news to Harry. Lori had to have someone to account for the pregnancy.

"Did she say who with?" he asked.

"Oh yes, and you're not going to believe it." Jess took a breath and looked round at their expectant faces. "Terry Blackwood."

There was a silence as they each processed what this meant.

"An affair is one thing, but the fact that she was seeing Blackwood puts a whole new slant on the case," she said. Those in the team who knew of Blackwood and his reputation agreed. Harry was just learning about the man, but already he had a bad feeling.

"And your big news?" Jess asked him.

"Lori's baby wasn't her husband's. I'm wondering now if it was Blackwood's, and if she'd told him of the pregnancy, how he'd have reacted," Harry said soberly.

"Badly, according to Debra," Jess said. "Blackwood has a wife and two teenage boys. He keeps his family life well away from his nefarious dealings and doesn't allow any crossover. As far as his close friends and relatives are concerned, the Blackwoods are pillars of the community. He wouldn't tolerate any rumours to the contrary."

"You think Lori might've threatened to tell the wife?"

Jess shrugged. "She may have done. The two women did know each other. Carla Blackwood runs the theatre group in Ryebridge and Lori was a member. But I imagine Blackwood would have warned Lori off, he wouldn't want his wife to know about the affair. We can only guess at whether he threatened violence if she said anything."

"But we do know what sort of man he is."

Jess looked at Harry. "Blackwood's no stranger to murder if that's what you mean. According to Debra, his wife Carla has a temper too, but Debra reckons that she wouldn't kill Lori, that would be taking things too far."

He looked at Jess. "You know what this means, we'll have to speak to Blackwood, and probably the wife as well."

Jess grabbed a pen and went up to the whiteboard. "It also means we now have three possible suspects, Adam Lansing and both Blackwood and his wife, Carla. We don't know that Lansing didn't find out and killed Lori in a fit of jealousy."

She was right, but which one of the three was most likely to go that far? One thing was for sure, Blackwood's name had come up. If he had been having an affair with Lori, and Debra wasn't simply stirring things, it certainly opened up the case.

"Debra told me something else," Jess announced. "He's got some new friends, people from the Radford hospital. He's been taking a lot of phone calls from there and she's no idea why."

"They may be supplying him with drugs," Col suggested.

"We'll keep an open mind for now. It might be nothing, but before we can discount it we need more information. Blackwood has some other new friends too, apart from those at the Radford, but Debra wouldn't say who."

Harry changed the subject. "Any theories about the way Lori was dressed? I'll admit I'm at a loss to figure out what all that Victorian garb means."

"I'm visiting that antique market tomorrow," Col reminded them. "I might strike lucky."

"Who, when, and a description of the buyer will do nicely," Jess said with a grin.

Harry turned to Constable Bob Tait. "Bob, you're going too, and make sure you wear plain clothes. We don't want the market traders doing a runner before we've had the chance to talk to them."

Meanwhile, that interview with Blackwood was a priority. Harry was well aware of how tricky it might be. He didn't know much about the man, but he had gleaned from the others something of his fearsome reputation, and he understood the need to tread carefully. It seemed Blackwood was a man used to getting his own way and wouldn't take kindly to being a suspect in a murder case. Harry also realised that it would be necessary to speak to his wife, and that could make things doubly difficult.

"Do we know where Blackwood is likely to be during the daytime?" he asked the others.

"He has an office at the Rainbow," Col said. "Want me to ring and see if he's there?"

"No, I prefer the element of surprise." He looked at Jess. "You up for this? A few questions, get a feel for the man behind the persona."

"No choice, have we?" she said. "Scary or not, it's got to be done. Anyway, there's every chance he won't be there. From what Debra told me, Blackwood's one busy man."

"We'll take that risk."

CHAPTER TWELVE

The atmosphere in the Rainbow felt different again, worse than on both Jess's previous visits, and those had been bad enough. There was no music for a start, and the place was deserted apart from two suited security men standing by the bar. The place felt intimidating, and Jess was immediately on edge. She stood behind Harry, wondering how long it would take them to make it to the exit if they had to run.

"We're shut," one of the men barked at them.

"Police." Harry waved his warrant card at him. "We'd like a word with Mr Blackwood."

"He's out."

Short, not very sweet and untrue. "You sure about that?" Harry asked. "Isn't that his flash sports car parked outside?"

"I said he's out," the man repeated slowly.

There was a distinct threat to his tone that made Jess shiver.

Harry moved several paces towards the bar. "I don't believe you. I think he's right here in his office. What's the problem? Has he got something to hide?"

"I'd leave now if I was you, while you can still walk."

"D'you know what you can get these days for threatening a police officer carrying out his duty?" Harry tutted.

"Now, are you going to tell Mr Blackwood I want to see him, or do I get a warrant and take a look around for myself?"

One of the security guards moved towards the pair, scowling. He was huge. Tall and bulky with a shaved head, his fists clenched at his sides.

Jess shrank back in fear. If this got nasty they stood no chance. Her mind went off at a wild tangent and she found herself wondering what piece of evidence she could leave behind to prove they'd been here. Something Hettie might find, she thought, fiddling with a loose button on her jacket cuff. She considered flicking it off into a corner of the room where, with luck, forensics would spot it.

"I wouldn't if I were you, mate," Harry said, pushing Jess behind him as they backed off. "This is intimidating a police officer. It can get you into big trouble."

"I'll take my chances. In any case, you won't be around to make a fuss. The pretty lady neither."

They continued their slow retreat. For what felt like hours, they both believed they were in real trouble. But it was only seconds before they heard another voice.

"Now now, Edward, that's no way to speak to our guests. We should be showing them some of the hospitality we're famous for at the Rainbow."

The man who'd entered the bar was tall, with the lean athletic body of a man who worked out. He had short, stylishly cut fair hair and was impeccably dressed in a designer suit, crisp shirt and silk tie.

"You wanted a word." He smiled at them and gestured to a table. "Please, sit down. Terry Blackwood. How can I help you?"

Jess was quite dazzled. She'd never met the man, and the photos she'd seen didn't do him justice. He was good looking — a right smoothie, in fact. She could understand how a young woman like Lori would fall for the charm.

"We're investigating the murder of Lori Lansing," Harry began. "You knew her, I believe."

"Lori, yes," he admitted straight away. "Lori and her husband, Adam, but only because our paths crossed at various community occasions. Murdered, you said. The poor man must be suffering terribly. I knew she was missing but I never thought it would end like that. I must go round and offer Adam my condolences, maybe there's something I can do to help."

He was good, Jess gave him that. If you didn't know about his reputation, you would be taken in by the concerned looks and thoughtful words. "What was the nature of your relationship with Lori?" she asked.

For a moment Blackwood stared at her, his expression blank, and then he shook his head vehemently. "There was no *relationship*, as you put it. The Lansings were acquaintances, nothing more. And no way could I have any sort of relationship with a woman other than my wife, if that's what you're hinting at." He laughed. "My Carla would kill me."

"Odd. We've been told different." The words were out before Jess could think.

She felt Harry nudge her leg under the table and knew at once she'd given Blackwood too much information. "We were in here last night and spoke to a number of people. I'm sure someone said you and Lori were close." Since she'd probably said too much already, she thought she might as well stir things up a bit more. Jess looked at one of the goons watching them from the bar. "It could have been one of those gentlemen over there, or someone who looked very like them."

She was lying and Blackwood knew it. The villain shook his head. "People are quick to point the finger. You see, for reasons I don't understand, people think the worst of me. They see the house, the car and this place and think I'm hard, a villain even." He looked from one to the other as if butter wouldn't melt. "Of course, nothing could be further from the truth. Still, years of living with these rumours and mud sticks. These days anything goes wrong in Ryebridge and the police beat a path to my door." He gave the pair a knowing smile. "The truth is I'm doing my level best for the community." He gave a sigh. "But still folk think the worst of me."

"By doing your best, you mean your loan company?" Jess asked.

"People need money, love. I provide a service. All I ask is that they keep to the repayment plan."

"You charge interest?"

"I'm not a charity." He smiled. "I try very hard to make life as easy as possible for my customers, but still they complain."

"Perhaps it's the company you keep," Harry said, nodding at the bouncers.

Blackwood turned to them and beckoned. The huge man who had threatened them earlier lumbered across and stood by the table. "This is Edward, he looks like a caveman but take my word for it, he's really a big softie underneath. I employ him and the others because they're effective. They are good at steering trouble away from our doors. People come here and get tanked up, fancy their chances, then one look at Edward and his colleagues and they quickly change their minds."

Edward gave a grunt.

"I suggest you look elsewhere for a solution to your murder. Lori Lansing did come here, but she always left in perfect health."

"When did you last see her?" Jess asked.

Blackwood looked at her for a moment. "It would have been earlier in the month. I don't recall the exact date but I certainly haven't seen her recently."

"Mr Blackwood, would you be prepared to give us a DNA sample?" Harry asked.

"Whatever for?"

"It would help to rule you out of our enquiries."

"There's no need, Inspector." He smiled. "A few years ago, I was wrongly arrested on some trumped-up charge and spent a night in the cells. My prints and DNA were taken then."

"In that case, you'll be in our records." Harry returned the smile. "Thanks for the heads up."

Jess got to her feet. It was time to go. The place, the company, were making her nervous. Even so, she remembered to pass Blackwood a card. "If you remember anything you think might be significant, do give us a ring."

CHAPTER THIRTEEN

Back in the car, they both heaved a sigh of relief. "He's not the father of Lori's baby," Harry said. "He was too casual about us checking his DNA."

"He doesn't know Lori was pregnant though, does he? In fact, before we let that one slip out we should tell Adam Lansing," Jess said.

Harry wasn't too sure. "He won't be happy. She'd not started the IVF programme and he's infertile, so it'll be plain to him that Lori was having an affair. Are we ready to let him know that yet?"

"I feel sorry for the man but the truth might sharpen his memory," Jess said. "Considering the possibility that Lori was seeing Blackwood might loosen his tongue." She thought for a moment. "Lori having an affair gives Adam Lansing a motive for murder. We have to accept that. He might have loved her deeply but the desire for revenge can run deep too. The need to strike out can be overwhelming."

"Okay, supposing we go with that for a moment," Harry said, repeating the issues with this theory that Col had voiced earlier. "Why'd he make all that fuss? Why virtually camp out at the police station, asking for help, after she disappeared? If he had killed his wife he'd have kept himself to himself, faded quietly away, surely?"

"I don't know. Perhaps he thought his behaviour would divert suspicion from him, make us think he couldn't be guilty."

"We need a few more facts before we do anything," Harry said. While Jess drove them back to the station, he rang Hettie at the Reid and asked her to check the foetal DNA with that of Blackwood's.

"Will do," she promised, "and one of your lot brought in a toothbrush belonging to Lori. I'll be able to confirm her identity for sure very soon."

That was good news, it'd stop any doubt Lansing might harbour about it not being her. He'd no sooner finished the call than his mobile rang again. It was Colin.

"Ryebridge General have been on," he told Harry. "An ambulance picked up a young woman from the woods at the back of the swimming pool car park. She's been beaten and is unconscious."

"Do we have an identity?"

"Debra Dobson. She works at the Rainbow."

The news made Harry's stomach churn. That hadn't taken Blackwood and his crew long, Jess was only speaking to her at lunchtime. She wasn't going to like this.

"Do Hettie and the forensic team know?" he asked.

"I plan to ring her next."

"Well, you do what needs to be done where she was found. Speak to Hettie, make sure she gathers every scrap of evidence she can find. Jess and I will go to the hospital, see if she's up to talking."

"Debra was still out of it according to the uniform who rang it in, so don't expect too much," Col said.

"I'll see you back at the station."

"Trouble?" Jess asked.

"Yes, Jessie, another victim, although this one is still alive. I think we've really upset the applecart this time.

Someone's getting nervous and lashing out." He went quiet, considering how to tell her the next bit. He knew Jess, and she was bound to blame herself. "The victim is Debra."

Jess turned pale. "Blackwood's people must have been watching us at the café." Her voice wavered. "I was afraid of that. We'll have been seen last night too. I made a point of speaking to Debra. I even gave her my card."

"We're not to blame. Getting upset won't do you or Debra any good. We'll give her the police protection she needs and carry on, find out who did this and make sure they pay."

"We know who did it, Harry. Perhaps not with his own fists but he's behind it. It'll be Blackwood."

"Evidence, Jessie. We can't do anything without it."

"He's one creepy man," she said. "All lightness and manners on the surface but deadly underneath. He's got no morals, no empathy, nothing touches him."

"If he's behind the murder of Lori and what's happened to Debra, we will get him. Have faith. After all, we've worked on more difficult cases. And you're wrong about nothing touching him. His wife, Carla, remember her. He's not keen for her to find out about the other women in his life."

"I doubt she's that daft, surely she must know."

"She's his Achilles heel, believe me, and when I've figured out how, we'll use it."

"Poor Debra, she didn't deserve this."

"Let's hope she recovers and gets her life back, such as it is. Blackwood is a bastard who's held this town in his grip for far too long. It's about time someone stood up to him and made him pay."

"That sounds like the start of a vendetta to me, Lennox."

"Don't worry, Jess. Whatever we decide to do, it'll be within the law."

They pulled into the hospital car park and made for the A & E reception desk. A nurse pointed them in the direction of a waiting area and told them the doctor would be along shortly.

Jess sat down, took her mobile from her pocket and texted Kyle. "Looks like it's going to be a late one. Shame, he had a meal booked at that new Italian place. Looks like we'll have to put it off until another night."

"You like him, don't you?" Harry said.

"He's okay and we get on. He's new to the area and doesn't know many people, so I don't want to let him down. He's a decent man. At least I've got someone. What about you, Lennox? What happened to that Scottish woman who visited last year?"

"Isla Stewart, you mean. She was engaged to my brother, Paul. Nothing to do with me."

Jess grinned. "You like her though. It was written all over your face."

"Well, okay, that might be, but there's no future for us. Sad but that's how it is. And I've got nothing else to say on the matter." Harry turned his face to the window.

"Still a touchy subject, I see, like everything else to do with your life in Scotland. I had hoped that one day you'd trust me enough to open up, tell me what happened to bring you skuttling south, where you obviously don't want to be."

Harry Lennox held up his hands with the scarred fingers. "This is what happened, Jess. I don't like talking about it, that's all."

Jess winced. Though healed, his fingers still looked a mess. She'd dearly love to know what really happened to cause those terrible scars. She'd heard his version of events, but the truth could well be something else entirely.

CHAPTER FOURTEEN

Debra Dobson had regained consciousness. She lay on her back, an oxygen mask over her face and one arm in a sling. When the pair approached, she opened her swollen, black eyes and groaned. Someone had given the poor woman a real going over.

A nurse was with her. "It looks worse than it is, superficial bruising mostly," she said. "The worst injury is the broken arm."

Jess sat down beside the bed. "I'm sorry, Debra, we're to blame for what's happened. You tried to help us and this is what you get."

Debra eased the mask from her face with her good arm and looked at Jess. "I knew what I was doing. I didn't have to meet you. I knew I was taking a risk, but someone has to stop Blackwood. I was in the alley that runs beside the club when the sod who did this came at me from behind. I didn't see who it was but I suspect it was one of Blackwood's goons. When he'd finished, he threw me into the back of a van, drove to the woods and left me." She coughed and took a sip of the water Jess offered her. "Can't smoke in here and I'm gagging for a fag." She struggled to sit up. "Where's my clothes?"

"In that bag on the chair." Harry nodded.

"Have a look in my jeans pocket," she told Jess. "I tried to fight off the bloke who attacked me. We grappled for a bit and I pulled something off his coat and slipped it into my pocket."

"Good move," Harry said, passing the garment to Jess. "Did you get a look at his face?"

"No, and anyway he had a balaclava over his head. He was a big bloke though, which is why I reckon it was one of them from the club."

"It won't happen again. There'll be police keeping a watch on you from now on," Jess assured her.

Debra looked doubtful. "Blackwood can get to anyone, anywhere, love. You've no idea. The man's got friends in high places and a lot of influence. I won't be so lucky next time either. This was a warning — keep out of his business or else. Next time he'll kill me."

The thing Debra had taken from her attacker was a badge. Jess examined it and handed it to Harry. "Some sort of football emblem, I think, but I don't recognise it."

Jess dropped it in the evidence bag Harry held out. "I recognise it. It's a Ryebridge Celtic badge," he said.

"Perhaps Blackwood's muscle are fans."

"What? That lot? Football fans? First I've heard of it," Debra said.

"Could it have been Blackwood himself who attacked you?" Harry asked.

"Doubtful. He usually dishes out the instructions, doesn't like to get his hands dirty. But make no mistake, he's handy with his fists and more than capable. You do know his reputation as a loan shark? What he does to folk who default on the repayments?"

Jess shook her head.

"Most of them live in rented property," Debra said. "There's an entire street full of Blackwood's customers down by the canal. Default on the rent and he gets the landlord to up the pressure, threatens to have them turfed out onto the street. There was an old man, Ken Venables, who had a house on there and owed Blackwood money. He pleaded with Blackwood to let him stay, but the crook was having none of it. He threw Venables out into the street himself, and had him beaten black and blue. Victoria Terrace is all but empty now, apart from a few brave souls who have virtually barricaded themselves in."

Harry put the evidence bag in his pocket. "No one has complained to us. Are you sure it's as bad as you say?"

"Yes, love, and as for complaining, no one would dare. Look what's happened to me. I reckon the only reason I'm not dead is because Blackwood is using me as a warning to anyone else who decides to take him on."

Food for thought. Harry decided to take a look at this place tomorrow, speak to people and weigh up what was going on for himself. While they were speaking, two unforms had arrived and were seated in the corridor outside Debra's room. Harry smiled at Debra. "Your bodyguards have arrived. You're quite safe now."

Jess stood up, and she and Harry prepared to leave. "You've got my number if you want to talk, but in any case we'll be back tomorrow to see if you've remembered anything else."

The pair made for the exit. "So, do we visit Lansing or not?" Harry asked.

"Might as well. The evening's ruined now anyway. Though don't expect any thanks for what we've got to tell him."

"I reckon he must have known Lori was unfaithful. She went out a great deal, liked the club, that theatre group, and had any number of young friends. It just follows, it's a natural train of thought."

"It might be an idea not to shove it down his throat. We might learn more," Jess said.

"Right from the start, Jess, my instincts have told me he's holding back."

"He really is high on your suspect list, isn't he? Well, I don't go for it. It's the fuss he made when Lori went missing. That doesn't add up to me. Why do it if he was responsible?"

Harry said nothing, just made for the car. Speaking to Lansing would be unpleasant enough, without Jess glaring daggers at him.

* * *

Lansing expressed outrage at Harry's suggestion that Lori had been unfaithful. "No way. I don't believe my Lori would do such a thing. Yes, I was older, but she always said she preferred it that way."

Jess felt sorry for the man. He couldn't take on board what Harry was telling him, she could see it in his face.

"Your wife was pregnant when she died," Harry told him. "If she wasn't having an affair, how d'you account for that?"

"We were going for IVF, perhaps she'd already started the treatment."

"She hadn't," Harry said bluntly. "Now what I need from you is information, any suspicions you may have of men Lori could have been seeing."

Lansing's face clouded over. Jess could see that he didn't like either Harry's tone or the suggestion he'd made. "It might help us find who killed her," she said kindly.

"You can do all that. Test the baby's DNA. Won't that tell you?"

"Only if the father's DNA is on record."

"Are you sure you don't know anything?" Jess asked him. "You want Lori's killer caught and we need all the help we can get."

Lansing hung his head. "I did suspect that there was someone. I thought as much when she kept buying all those new clothes. She was never at home, always out with one mate or another. When I asked her about it, she got angry and clammed up."

"And you've no idea who it was?" Jess said.

"No, and I blame myself. I tended to be protective of Lori and she didn't like it. I know that sometimes I came across as the heavy-handed husband. If I'm honest, I was terrified of losing her and I didn't want to put her under too much pressure."

"Shame," Harry said. "If you'd got more involved with her friends and where she went nights, you might have saved her life."

Jess thought the comment harsh. Lansing was barely holding it together as it was. "We'll leave you now. We get any more information, you'll be the first to know."

CHAPTER FIFTEEN

Wednesday

Gabby French slid the bolt on the front door shut and turned the key in the lock. The windows back and front were barricaded with offcuts of wood Arthur Bates, the joiner, had given her. Preparation done, they were here for the duration. A scary thought, and not one Gabby wanted to dwell on. She had to believe she'd win, that Blackwood would see sense and back off.

But would he? Blackwood and the landlord, Jack Leyburn, had sent the heavies round yesterday. They'd gone door to door demanding full repayment of the money the residents had borrowed off Blackwood over the years, and the rent owed to Leyburn. Gabby had got into debt when she'd fallen pregnant with Ollie. Time off work and then maternity leave had sounded the death knell for her job. She'd had no idea where her neighbours had gone, but this morning the street was eerily quiet. No one was about except old Mrs Hardy, who was now huddled over Gabby's one-bar electric fire, whispering to herself. The poor old lady had no one and didn't understand what was happening. Two years ago, she'd borrowed fifty quid from Blackwood, and now, what with the interest along with penalties for late repayments, owed him well over a grand. Terrified of what was to come, she had banged on Gabby's door at two this morning, asking for help. What could she do? The woman was desperate. The alternative was to see her harmed by Blackwood's thugs.

They'd all agreed to stick together. All the houses on Victoria Terrace were rented from Leyburn, a close friend of Blackwood's who'd threatened to evict anyone who didn't pay up. Harold Williams from next door had gone to the Help Centre on the shopping precinct to get advice, anything they could use to fight the situation. But he didn't come back hopeful. The rental agreements were in black and white, written in favour of the landlord, not the tenants. Fighting their corner would cost money, and the advisor had suggested they try to strike a bargain with Leyburn. That wouldn't work. Blackwood was the one pulling the strings.

The villain was a moneylender with no scruples. The people on this street were helpless, they had nothing, no resources. Over the years they'd all borrowed money from him despite the extortionate terms. Often the first loan had been the deposit on the rent for one of these houses. Gabby didn't know what had happened to make Blackwood suddenly turn on them all, but she was afraid it had something to do with her brother, Dillon.

He worked for Blackwood and reckoned that if he got something on the villain, it would make him think twice about taking action against the tenants. That was two days ago, and she hadn't seen him since. Something else to worry about. Dillon had a big mouth, he lost his temper easily, which wouldn't go down well with the moneylender or his mob. He also had a heroin addiction that ruled his life.

So here they were, the last bastion of Victoria Terrace's rebellion against Blackwood's villainy and Leyburn's terror. A teenage mother of a sickly infant and a batty old woman in the early throes of dementia. Some army to set against that pair and their thugs.

Gabby had met Blackwood a few times. She was reluctant to admit it to anyone, but he was a cousin of her dead mother's. Not that the relationship cut any ice with him. He hadn't had anything to do with his family in years. Still, each time she'd seen him, Gabby had enjoyed bringing it up, teasing him about his background, reminding him that it was just as lowly as hers. All it did was anger him. She'd even rung him, asking for time to repay, reminding him that she was family, but it made no difference. Pay now or suffer the consequences were the words he lived by. In desperation, she'd turned to Leyburn but he'd offered nothing constructive either. It appeared that he too was in hock to Blackwood and would do as he was told.

Gabby looked at the tiny bundle in the sling and wondered if the time had come to try the housing office again — not that it'd done much good in the past.

She was jolted back into reality by the rattle of a van as it trundled along the cobbled street. They were coming. Almost at once, Ollie, who'd been sleeping peacefully, started to scream and cough. He wasn't well, and had things been normal, they would have been at the doctor's surgery this morning.

There was more noise. She peered through a chink between the wooden slats covering the window. A group of men stood in the middle of the road. They were a grim looking bunch, shouting and swearing, each with an axe in his hands. Blackwood couldn't do this, surely he must realise that there were vulnerable people living in these houses.

* * *

The team had an early meeting to go over what they had so far. "We've got theories aplenty but not many facts," Harry said. "We're waiting on Hettie's team to come back with some DNA results. Hopefully, these will answer a couple of outstanding questions. The first one — is the body that of Lori Lansing? Second, was Terry Blackwood the father of her unborn child?"

"Even if he is, what can we do?" Col asked.

"It gives him a motive for her murder, his jealous wife too," Jess said.

"And if he isn't?" Col said.

Jess shook her head. "Of course he is." Harry might believe that Blackwood wasn't the father, but he was very much in the frame as far as she was concerned. "Blackwood is the man Lori was seeing. No one has even hinted that there was anyone else, not even Debra, her mate, and I am sure she would know."

Col stood up with a nod to Bob. "I'll leave you two to argue the toss. We're off to deepest Cheshire and that antiques fair. Wish us luck. If we get anything, I'll be straight on the phone."

"It's a long shot," Harry said once they'd gone. "Crowds of people, and that clothing could have been bought anytime."

"Who do we chase after today?" Jess asked, her eyes on the incident board. "We've nothing on Lansing or the Blackwoods that we can make a case of. That dead end we're knocking our heads against is harder to breach than ever."

Ignoring her comment, Harry said, "I fancy taking a look at some of the streets Blackwood is terrorising. Speak to people, see what the residents have to say."

"I shouldn't think they'll be happy. They're in debt to the man and there's no let-up. Men like Blackwood will take everything they've got and then some."

Harry looked at Jess with his jaw set firm and an odd expression on his face. The idea of Blackwood bullying people in no position to fight back bothered him. "Why do people do it? Why borrow from him? They know what he's like."

"People get desperate, Harry. Lenders like Blackwood are the last resort, but borrowing from him does give them a little breathing space. The problems come later when they can't pay."

"Let's see what some of his customers have to say and go from there."

"You really do have it in for him, don't you?" she said.

"He's a wicked man, Jessie, and he's getting away with it because he has people beaten up, even murdered. And I want to be the one to bring him down."

"I feel much like you," Jess said, "but we have to tread careful. You said it yourself, we stay within the law. No taking risks. I'll drive and you can use the time to cool down, get a grip and lose the anger. We'll start with those streets by the canal."

She was right. He was getting far too wound up about the case, and about Blackwood in particular. As they were leaving, Harry had a word with one of the uniforms. "While we're gone, do some asking around and see if anyone has complained about Blackwood's moneylending activities."

CHAPTER SIXTEEN

The pair pulled onto the cobbles of Victoria Terrace and came to a grinding halt behind a large van. They watched a group of men going door to door, shouting and banging. Harry saw a large, stocky bloke take a swing at one with an axe he was carrying.

"Hey, stop that!" he shouted.

Harry leaped out of the car and rushed over to him. "Police. What d'you think you're doing?"

The man just grinned. "Getting rid of the rubbish, and that'll include you, Mr Policeman, if you don't do one."

Harry looked back at Jess, who was already on her mobile — he hoped, ringing for backup. "You can't do this. There are people living in these houses."

"They pay what they owe, especially the one who lives here, and we'll leave. Refuse, and they're on the streets. I've got authority from the landlord to evict the bloody lot of them."

"Back off or I'll arrest you," Harry said.

The bloke, a thick-set stocky man, gave a loud laugh and shook his fist in Harry's face. "Do that, Mr Policeman, and you won't make it back to your car."

Harry looked at Jess again who gave him a nod. "Okay, but surely we can talk about this, calm things down." He was playing for time, hoping the troops would get here quick. He didn't fancy taking this one on, he was bound to come off worst. All he could do was keep him sweet until help arrived. "Who're you working for? I'll give him a ring, see if we can't come to an agreement."

"Sod off, I've got a job to do."

The stocky bloke raised his axe, ready to strike at the front door again, when police sirens could be heard coming round the corner.

Suddenly an older man stepped between them, shaking his fists. "There's folk in that house," he shouted. "A young lass, a bairn, and the old woman from further up."

"Calm down, I'm police." Harry showed him his identity badge. The man with the axe swore at the pair of them and sloped off back to the rest of the group.

"Arthur Bates. I live at the end house and I'm a friend of the lass that's caused all this bother. She got on the wrong side of Blackwood, borrowed money and can't pay it back. This is what he does, the man's an animal. You won't stop him. Once you lot go, these thugs will be back."

Harry looked around. A number of uniformed officers were rounding up the men with axes and herding them into a police riot van. "We'll take the lot to the station and leave a presence here," he told Arthur.

"Can't stay here for ever though, can they? Someone should sort that villain out, and his friend the landlord. The pair of them need fixing once and for all."

Harry was about to reply when a man in a suit carrying a clipboard hurried up to them. "Those men were carrying out orders," he said. "You've no right to cart them off like that."

"They were threatening the residents, and I dread to think what would have happened if we hadn't turned up."

"Mr Leyburn, the landlord, and Mr Blackwood, are not going to take kindly to your actions. Be warned, there will be consequences."

The man turned on his heel and walked off, mobile clamped to his ear. Minutes later he was back, shaking his head. "Blackwood say's that bitch in yon house needs to understand the way things are. She pays what she owes today, or she vacates the property. She owes rent too, and the landlord has new tenants lined up with the deposit ready to hand over."

"A deposit borrowed from Blackwood no doubt," Arthur said angrily. "And so the spiral continues."

Harry looked at the dilapidated houses, the loose-fitting windows and sagging gutters, and shook his head. "I doubt she'd stay here if she had any choice. She's probably tried and found the housing situation around here as tricky as I have."

"Not our problem. The landlord won't have it. He and Blackwood want their money. She hands over what she owes or she goes, and it's my job to make sure she does one or the other."

* * *

Gabby French could barely believe what was going on out in the street. After a deal of shouting and bustle, thankfully Blackwood's thugs were now under control. The person calling the shots at the moment was a tall blond man, handsome with a chiselled jaw and high cheekbones. Not someone Gabby had seen in this neck of the woods before.

It looked safe enough to go outside. She wanted to thank the man and find out what would happen next.

He smiled and came over to her. "DI Harry Lennox, Ryebridge CID. You're the cause of all this, so I'm told."

Not a comment Gabby appreciated. "Told by who? That gangster, Blackwood? The truth is the landlord, Leyburn, wants us all out so he can sell the land. He and Blackwood cooked this up between them." Seeing that he knew nothing about this, she smiled at him. "Sorry, it's not your fault. You have just saved the lot of us. I'm Gabby French and this is Ollie." She planted a kiss on the infant's head.

"I'm Harry and this is DS Jess Wilde," he said.

Gabby nodded. "You seem to know who I am already. Word gets around quick when you're a troublemaker."

"Are there many people left in these houses?" A policewoman approached them.

"Me and my infant son, Ollie, live here. Old Mrs Hardy lives two doors up but she's way past understanding what's going on. Arthur, the joiner, who you've just been speaking to, has a house at the end. It's the one with a large garage attached that he uses as a workshop."

The infant was coughing and crying his little heart out.

"Is he okay?" Harry asked.

"He's like the rest of us, scared stiff. Babies pick up on things. Besides, he isn't well."

"D'you have anywhere else to go, family for instance? Friends?" Jess asked.

Gabby shook her head. "If I had, d'you think I'd stay in this dump? You've no idea what it's like, but what choice do I have? The only family I have is a brother, Dillon, who's high as a kite most days. He went off to get us some help twenty-four hours ago and I haven't seen him since. I doubt I will now. He'll keep away until all this has died down. Most folk I hung out with gave up on me when I fell for this little bundle and the father didn't want to know. I was six months gone and living rough then I met one of Blackwood's people. He said I could borrow whatever I needed to make a new start and repay the money once I got on my feet. He even showed me this house and said I could get it at a special rent for the first few weeks." She looked at Jess. "I had nothing else and was desperate. What would you have done?"

"Social Housing?" Jess suggested. "There's an office on the precinct."

"D'you know how many people round here clamour at their doors each day, asking for help? I don't stand a chance."

"But you have an infant."

Doris Hardy chose that moment to put in an appearance. She stood in the doorway of Gabby's house and called out, "Anyone making a pot of tea? A nice hot cuppa and I'll get back to my own house."

"She's off her head," Gabby told them. "Arthur reckons it's dementia. There were people wandering around up and down the street in the dark last night and the noise scared her, that's why she came to mine."

"If you don't want to approach the social housing people, what will you do now?" Jess asked.

"Stay put. We've nowhere else to go. Mrs Hardy is vulnerable and my Ollie's ill. I can't cope with tramping around looking for somewhere else, it's all doing my head in."

"We'll get you some help," Jess promised.

Gabby could see from the detective's face that she meant well but she also knew she had no clue how hard that would be. They just didn't get it. Another pitying face, another do-gooder full of promises. Over the last month Gabby had tried everywhere and come up blank. "Social Housing will stick us in a B & B and I don't want that. Everyone in there will scream all night for Ollie to be quiet. He's a crier, nothing I can do about it."

They were joined again by the woman police officer. "These people need urgent help with accommodation," Harry told her. "See what you can do but no B & Bs. Gabby here needs somewhere more permanent and Mrs Hardy needs assessing to work out what is best for her. While you do that, would you leave someone at the house to make sure they stay safe?"

Nice idea but would it work? Gabby doubted it. She had already been told there was nowhere, and anyway, she already had a place to live.

"Can I go home now?" she asked Jess. "It's cold out here and Ollie is shivering."

"We'll leave people here," Harry reassured her. "There should be no more trouble today."

Jess wasn't listening, her eyes were glued to her mobile.

"This might explain why Leyburn is so keen to get you out," she said. "A message from a colleague at the station. It appears that Leyburn wants to clear the houses and sell the land."

Gabby pointed to a sealed-off factory building several hundred metres away. "That's what I said. I know what he wants to do but the land is worth nowt. See the factory over there, the one with the high fence all around it? Well, it used to be the old chemical works. All the land about here is contaminated. Knock this lot down and it'll cost a packet to clean it up. Whatever Leyburn and Blackwood have cooked up between them, I doubt it's got anything to do with redevelopment."

CHAPTER SEVENTEEN

The pair went back to the car. "D'you want to find Leyburn and have a word?" Jess asked. "He needs to understand that he can't just turf his tenants out into the street on Blackwood's say-so."

"Might do some good, might not. They'll all have a lease, Jess, but I doubt it gives them much protection. What's the betting there are clauses in it giving Leyburn the right to do what he pleases. It's a classic example of a dodgy landlord preying on people's need. Gabby said herself that she took the house on when she was desperate."

"What happened back there was horrifying. If we hadn't turned up they could all have been hurt, young Gabby and her baby for starters. It doesn't bear thinking about. Leyburn has an office on Ryebridge High Street. I think we should mark his card."

Harry wasn't going to argue with her. He was furious about the whole business himself. He couldn't stand men like Leyburn and Blackwood who presumed they could ride roughshod over the law and do as they pleased to innocent people. He took a deep breath. Speaking to Leyburn while he was still so angry wouldn't work, he had to calm down, deal with Leyburn professionally.

"How come these men have become so powerful? Why didn't we see it happening?" Jess asked.

"It happened when we weren't looking," Harry said. "We try, Jess. We do the best we can to keep this town trouble free, but we're a long way from succeeding. Look at the drug dealing we have to contend with. That's a business that's growing every day."

"People like Leyburn and Blackwood prey on the weak and needy like Gabby and the others on that street. Blackwood lent her money knowing full well she'd never be able to repay it."

They were heading towards the High Street when Harry's mobile rang. It was Hettie from the Reid, so he put her on speaker phone.

"I can confirm that the young woman found dead in the old-fashioned clothing was Lori Lansing," she told him. "The DNA I managed to get from her toothbrush proved conclusive. However, Terry Blackwood was not the father of her unborn child."

Harry looked at Jess and nodded. "Knew it. What did I say?"

"There is something else," Hettie said. "But Melanie wants to tell you about that herself, it's rather complicated. Can you come in?"

"Perhaps the Reid and then Jack Leyburn?" Jess suggested.

"Be with you shortly," he said and finished the call. He looked at Jess. "There. I suspected all along that the father wasn't Blackwood, he was too blasé about the DNA."

"But it does give us another problem. If not Lansing and not Blackwood, who was Lori sleeping with? There's been no mention of anyone else."

"We go through that list of friends again and this time we push for answers. She was seeing someone and one of them has to know who," Harry said.

Jess made a face. "All I know is that this case gets no easier. We've gone from the murder of a young woman to a dodgy landlord, with a brutal moneylender thrown in. I wonder what delights Melanie has turned up for us."

* * *

Melanie had given instructions for the pair to be shown straight to her office once they arrived. She sat behind her desk, a report and an array of images in front of her.

"I owe you an apology," she began. "I should have noticed it the first time round but I didn't. I can only put that down to tiredness. The day I did the post-mortem on Lori Lansing, I'd been working through the night. As you know, the missing kidneys and unexpected pregnancy were the highlights of the post-mortem. What with that, the slight decomposition and the terrible beating her head and face took, I missed it."

This wasn't like Melanie. She was first class at her job and rarely had reason to apologise for anything. "Just spit it out," Harry urged. "Whatever it is, no one is going to lay the blame at your feet."

She shot him a look. "This is hard for me. I did my best at the time but I can't help feeling my efforts were somewhat slapdash."

Harry smiled at her. "Never. We know you're the best, Melanie."

Dismissing his words with a wave of her hand, she continued. "First off, we've had the results of certain tests back. Lori was not a regular drug user. I did wonder if she might be, given how skinny she was but that wasn't the case. Also, the splinters of wood are ash, so I'd say a baseball bat was used in the beating. Now for the important bit. Lori's eyes. Recall how I said they were missing? When I did the post-mortem, I thought that was most likely down to the wildlife where she'd been left." She shook her head. "But I was wrong."

"What are you saying?" Jess asked. "Are you suggesting that her killer took them?"

Melanie nodded. "I now believe they were surgically removed — well, a knife was used in any event."

82

The two detectives looked at each other. Neither could get their head round what she'd told them. Finally, Harry spoke. "Surgically? Not just flicked out with a knife or some other implement to keep as a trophy for instance, horrific as that sounds?"

His description made Jess wince.

"No," Melanie said. "I've magnified the wounds and can see where decomposition has begun, but I can also see that there is a sharp edge where the eye was cut out. If it had been done hurriedly, the wound would be less defined, more, er, ragged."

"When you say surgically, you're talking about a doctor then," Harry said. "What could they do with her eyes?"

"Not necessarily a doctor," Melanie said, "but a sharp knife, possibly a scalpel, was used and care taken to remove the entire eye."

"Who would want to do that?" Jess asked. "Why take her eyes?"

Harry said thoughtfully, "It could be connected to why her killer tried so hard to obliterate her face. He didn't want us to identify her. You know, eye colour and all that."

But Melanie had a different explanation. "Given that her kidneys were removed and the eyes too, they could have been taken for spare-part surgery."

The notion was horrific. Jess turned to Harry and shook her head. "We have nothing like that going on in Ryebridge. Surely, we'd know about it if it was."

"It has to start somewhere, Jess," Harry said, grimly.

He nodded at Melanie. "Thanks. Awful as it is, this might help us in some way."

The two left Melanie's office, each deep in thought.

* * *

"What about the husband?" Jess asked. "Do we tell him?"

"Not yet," Harry said.

"D'you want to go back to the station and bring the team up to speed?" Jess asked as they pulled away from the Reid.

"Not yet, we've still got to interview Jack Leyburn."

"It's just gone lunchtime, so with luck he'll be at his office on the High Steet," Jess said.

"What Melanie has just told us, the implications are huge," Harry said after a while. "We're going to have to investigate the black market in organ selling, or worse, people being killed to supply a need. That means getting onto the people based in Manchester Central who have the up-to-date info on such things."

"Will they interfere in our case?" she asked.

"I'm not sure," he replied.

The cogs started rolling. Jess recalled something Debra Dobson had told her. "There is something. It might not mean much, but Debra told me that Blackwood has some new friends, people who work at that private clinic, the Radford. She's no idea what's going on, she thought it might be a drugs thing, but perhaps it's this."

Harry nodded. "We'll make some discreet enquires. And quick, before we're faced with anything else."

CHAPTER EIGHTEEN

Leyburn kept the two detectives waiting in the reception area for a good fifteen minutes. Harry was starting to lose it by the time his PA called them through to his office.

"Sorry about the delay," he said. "A small emergency at home. Fortunately, I've managed to get things under control over the phone. All the housekeeper has to do now is follow my instructions."

Harry wasn't interested in hearing about his private life and made no comment. But Leyburn did look like a man at the end of his tether. He was in his shirt sleeves, seated behind a huge oak desk with a mobile in front of him. He was in his early forties, tall and heavily built. He was physically a match for Blackwood, that was for sure.

"Your tenants on Victoria Terrace," Harry began. "If we hadn't been there this morning, someone could have been seriously hurt or even killed."

Leyburn flushed a deep beetroot red. "A misunderstanding. That was not meant to happen. Speak to the tenants, I told those men. My orders were to make them see reason, try to find out why the rents on all those houses is consistently late. Unfortunately, the operatives who attended on my behalf got a little too . . . enthusiastic."

"They were thugs, Mr Leyburn," Jess said bluntly. "Thugs working for both you and Terry Blackwood, who's a friend of yours we're told."

"Look, Terry is eager to get back what they owe him, me too. I can't afford to carry those people. I've got prospective tenants with money in their pockets waiting to move in. To be honest, I'm losing patience with them. There are times when I think that Terry has the right idea."

"He's as much of a thug as those bullyboys he employs."

"It's just business, Detective," Leyburn said dismissively.

Harry leaned on Leyburn's desk, head close to his. "Business it might be, but anyone gets hurt on that street and I'll throw the book at you."

Just then, Leyburn's mobile rang. He snatched it up, listened intently for several minutes and got to his feet. "I've got to go. Sorry, the situation at home is worse and I'm needed. We'll have to do this some other time."

Leyburn got to his feet, grabbed his jacket and swiftly strode out of the office. Within seconds his PA came in.

"Mr Leyburn left his apologies and suggests you make an appointment for another day," she said.

"What's wrong at home? His wife ill?" Jess asked.

"His son, I'm afraid," she said. "The lad has diabetes and has had a hypo. Mrs Leyburn wants to get him to the hospital urgently."

"Ryebridge General?"

"No, the Radford, off Mottram Road." She smiled. "Only the best for young Jamie."

Harry saw the look of sympathy on Jess's face. The last thing he wanted was her getting all wrapped up in Leyburn's private life and feeling sorry for him. "Time we left," he said. "Tell Leyburn we'll be back." To Jess, he said, "That update you were talking about earlier, we should get on with it."

"He couldn't help bailing," she said as they made their way outside. "You heard him, his son's ill. And he didn't know we were coming."

"We need answers, Jess, and try as we might, we're not getting any. We're no further forward in finding out who killed Lori Lansing or why than the day her body was discovered."

"We have three candidates for prime suspect. We just need more evidence," she said. "Plus, we need to know if she was killed with the purpose of harvesting her organs, or was there some other motive."

"We're not getting the evidence though, are we?"

"It's no good getting stressed about it," she said. "And taking it out on me won't help either."

She was right. "I'm sorry, but getting involved in Leyburn's domestic issues isn't the answer."

* * *

The pair arrived back in the incident room at the same time as Col and Bob. Harry could tell from the look on their faces that they'd had no luck.

"There are hundreds of stalls, and at least twenty of them were selling that type of old-fashioned gear. We asked, flashed the photos, but not one of them recognised those clothes," Col said.

"It was worth a try," Harry said. "The way our luck's going, I half expected it anyway."

"One of the traders did make a suggestion though," Bob Tait said. "He said that the clothing could be part of a theatre wardrobe."

Jess looked at Harry. "We should have realised. There is a local theatre group, with Carla Blackwood calling the shots."

Jess had a valid point. "In that case, we need a word with Mrs Blackwood," Harry said to her. "This has opened up another avenue of investigation and I'd like to get a handle on it straightaway. Before we call it a day, we'll go and have a word."

Harry went up to the front of the room and stared at the board. It was crowded with facts, names and faces, but none of it added up to a suspect they could charge. He added the word 'theatre' followed by a question mark, turned and said to Col, "Apart from Carla, do we know who the other members of this group are?"

While Harry was talking, Col had been busy on his computer. "Carla Blackwood is the leading light. She recruits her actors mostly from the Baxendale and has invested time and a good deal of money into resurrecting the company after years of stagnation. Now they are a vibrant part of the Ryebridge social scene and most nights open to sizable audiences."

"We'll speak to her, show her the photos of the costume and see how she reacts," Harry said.

"Perhaps we should tread carefully with this one," Jess suggested. "Given her history, it might be better not to storm in. We might learn more with a softer approach."

Harry knew she was right. If that was what it took, so be it. He checked his watch. It was late in the afternoon. "Anyone have a contact number for the woman?"

"Your best bet is the theatre itself," Col said. "Currently they're rehearsing their latest play. It opens within the week, I've seen it advertised in the local paper."

"We'll have a quick word, then call it a day," Harry said to Jess.

The look on her face said it all, she wasn't happy. Missing out on another date with Kyle, he guessed.

CHAPTER NINETEEN

When they arrived there was a dress rehearsal in progress. Carla Blackwood had left for the day but luckily the pair caught her assistant, a woman called Anna Noble, who was calling the shots. She told the cast to have a break, eyed the detectives up and down and beckoned them to follow her into a poky office behind the stage.

Harry took the photo of the clothing Lori had been found in from his wallet. "Would you look at this and tell me if you recognise the clothing."

Anna Noble studied the image closely. "Oh yes, I recognise that all right. Caused a right to-do, that costume did."

"You're sure it's the same one?" Jess asked.

"I'd know it anywhere. The pleating and those pearl buttons on the bodice are distinctive."

"Can you tell us what happened to the costume?" Jess asked.

"It got coffee spilt on it. Lori Lansing occasionally took a part, but mostly her role was that of wardrobe mistress. That particular outfit was to be worn by young Paula Rushton. We were having a full-dress rehearsal and Paula spilled a mug of coffee down the frock. We were all very upset. Carla had sourced the costume specially for the play. Delicate as the fabric was, Paula had no choice but to take the whole lot away and wash it."

"Not Lori?"

Anna Noble shook her head. "She agreed to help her, the two were friends. The agreement was that if Paula got it washed, Lori would iron it. Those tucks down the front were tricky."

"Given that the outfit wasn't returned, didn't you wonder what had happened to it?" Jess asked.

"That's the thing. We never saw either of the girls or the outfit again after they took it. Carla tried ringing them but got nowhere, and then there was that terrible kidnap business with Lori so we just gave up."

"How did you know about that?" Jess asked. "We were given to understand that her husband kept it quiet."

Anna smiled. "I know Adam well, and he confided in me. He was in bits and needed someone to talk to. I told him to come to you lot but he put it off until the last minute. I know he blames himself for what happened to her."

"What about Paula Rushton?"

"After the costume incident we couldn't find her either, and her boyfriend was no help. He claimed he'd no idea where she was. Personally, I reckon she sold the stuff and has been keeping out of the way since." Anna Noble stuck her nose in the air.

"Has Paula tried to contact any of the cast, left messages? Anything?" Jess asked.

Anna thought for a moment then shook her head. "If she has, no one has said anything to me. Paula has missed so many rehearsals that even if she does turn up, she's out of the production this time round."

"Didn't it occur to you to ask her family where she was, or report her missing to the police?"

"I'm afraid I've been too busy."

"What about the clothes?" Harry asked.

"Who knows? Sold or still with Paula, which wouldn't surprise me. She and Lori joined our troupe not because they liked acting or were particularly good at it, it was the dressing-up that appealed to them. Like kids with a dressing-up box they were, Lori in particular. She loved the costumes and that one in particular. The times I've found her in the dressing room flouncing about in that dress or one very like it. The problem was, she didn't realise how valuable some of them are. That outfit, for example, Carla sourced it from a contact at a museum in Morecambe that was closing down." She smiled at the pair. "When we're doing an historical play, we like our costumes to be as authentic as possible. Her contact gave her all the stuff in your photos, plus three even more elaborate gowns."

"We really need a word with Paula," Jess said.

Anna shrugged. "Well, she isn't here. As I said, I haven't seen her since the day of the coffee incident. I don't know if any of the others have but they haven't told me. I've tried ringing her but had no luck."

"Address," Harry said sharply. He wasn't buying this, it was all too convenient.

"I have her details in the office, I'll get them for you."

"Before you go, did you know Lori Lansing well?" Jess asked.

Anna thought for a moment then shrugged. "Only as a member of the theatre group, not socially. She was a likeable young woman though, easy to take to."

"We're investigating her murder," Harry said. "Lori's husband is a member of the golf club, and we think there may be a link between the Blackwoods and the Lansings. Has Carla ever mentioned them?"

"Not to me, you'll have to ask Carla about them." She stared at the pair for a few moments. "Murder, you said. How dreadful. The photo you showed me of our costume, how does that fit in?"

Jess glanced at Harry. "I'm afraid that when Lori's body was found, she was wearing the outfit, right down to the wig."

"I shouldn't think Carla will want it back in that case." Anna's voice broke. "This could be disastrous for the theatre group."

91

"You do understand why we need to speak to Paula, don't you, and Carla too," Harry said. "Is Carla due back here today?"

"No, she went dashing off at lunchtime, some panic to do with her husband's business she said."

Harry knew exactly what that was about, the incident at Victoria Terrace earlier.

Anna scribbled Paula's details on a piece of paper and handed it to Jess. "Murder. I am sorry. I hope you find Paula soon. She got on people's nerves here, but we didn't wish her any harm."

"Would you tell Mrs Blackwood that we called and that we'll be in touch," Harry said.

* * *

They pulled out of the car park. "One last call," Harry said. "A quick word with Paula Rushton and then we'll call it a day."

"No one's seen her in weeks, so how are we supposed to find her now?"

"We'll nip round to her address, get the lie of the land and speak to the neighbours if any are around."

"I'm supposed to have a date tonight," Jess complained. "At this rate, Kyle won't want to know."

"If he likes you, he'll understand. You're a copper, late nights come with the job."

"But not every night. We still haven't made it to that new Italian place he promised to take me to."

Harry was only half listening. He had every sympathy with Jess, but it was a familiar story. The personal life of a detective could get messy — as he knew only too well.

"I explained how it would be when we started going out, but actually living it is something else." Jess sighed. "We'll meet up later, too late to do much with the evening and he'll have that look on his face, the disappointed one I hate so much."

"This is it," Harry said, ignoring her, and turning into a wide avenue.

Jess nodded, scowling. Paula lived on the Baxendale Estate on the outskirts of Ryebridge. It had a bad reputation that got no better as time went by.

Harry pointed to the tower block. "The way the numbers work, I reckon it'll be one of those on the first floor."

"Poor girl, can't be much fun living round here."

Minutes later the pair were on the deck, Harry banging on Paula's front door. There was no answer and the curtains were pulled shut.

"She's not been around in ages," said a male voice.

Harry turned round to see a young man, his gaunt face half hidden beneath a hood. He was skinny and from what little he could see of his eyes, he had the haunted look of a habitual user. He was probably in his mid-twenties and stared at the ground as he spoke.

"Who're you anyway? Someone wanting money? Cos if you are, you're out of luck."

Harry flashed his warrant card. "I want a word with Paula and it's important."

On seeing Harry's ID, the lad took several steps back. "She's not done owt wrong, not Paula. You're barking up the wrong tree there, mate."

"And you are?"

"Noel Tomkins," he said, averting his eyes. "Me and Paula, we've been going out for months. She's okay, she's not the type to break the law, but she doesn't always choose the best mates to hang out with, if you get my drift."

"Not really, Noel. Would you like to expand on that?" Harry said.

"She's been hanging around with a dealer from Salford. He's a bad lot. You lot must have stuff on him. Wilson's his name."

"At the moment it's Paula we're interested in," Harry said. "We think she has information that might be useful to us, so if you know where she is, we'd be grateful if you could tell us."

"I haven't seen her for weeks. The last time was when that Blackwood woman gave her a tongue-lashing about some daft dress that got coffee spilled on it." He was silent for a moment or two, trying to think, apparently. "It was about four weeks back. Ryebridge Celtic was playing at home in a friendly against Ashton. Paula was in a bad mood cos I wanted to go and watch the game. We had a shouting match out there on the spare ground. After that she marched off towards the launderette on the precinct with a bag of clothes. I keep asking around but no one has seen her since that day."

Jess was surprised. That game happened a while ago. "And you really have no idea what's happened to her?"

"No, and it's doing my head in. I have reported her missing but nowt's been done yet. You're the first coppers I've seen round here. It'll be like I said, she'll be lying low with that Wilson bloke. He was throwing his money around back then, always a big attraction where Paula's concerned."

"D'you have a photo of her?" Harry asked.

Noel took his mobile from his pocket and showed Harry an image of a smiling young woman with dark hair.

Harry handed him a card with his details on it. "Text me a copy of the photo and I'll put a call out to all our officers. They'll try to find her."

"Paula's never done anything like it before. She usually rings me as much as half a dozen times a day, but these last weeks there's been nowt. I've tried her mobile umpteen times but it's dead."

"We'll do our best," Harry promised. "Are you able to get inside her flat?"

"No, she only had the one key and I suppose she has that on her."

"We'll send some people round to take a look. I'll keep you posted." Harry smiled at him.

"D'you know what happened to the clothes she took to the launderette?" Jess asked.

The young man shrugged. "Disappeared with her, I suppose. Must have done, cos they haven't turned up." Tomkins walked off.

"What did you make of him?" Harry asked.

"He doesn't like talking to the police much, but round here that's to be expected," Jess said.

"He was shifty, nervous, and I'm wondering why," Harry said.

"What d'you think has happened to Paula?" Jess asked.

"I think we've got another missing woman, and it's already several weeks since she disappeared."

"Missing as in the other mispers, or like Lori?" Jess said.

"I hope not like Lori."

"Station?"

"Yeah, and then you can go and meet your Kyle. I'll bring the board up to date and get things moving."

CHAPTER TWENTY

Jess sat opposite Kyle Stanton in the restaurant, watching him scan the menu. She smiled. "Anything for me, I'm starving. I've hardly had a bite to eat all day." Jess was determined to have a good time this evening. Harry and she had had the day from hell and she deserved some downtime.

"He works you too hard," Kyle said.

"Harry's okay. The job gets under his skin, that's all. He's a good detective, gets results, and that's what matters. Besides, I'm every bit as keen as he is. Our current case is tricky." She tapped the side of her head. "Lots of brain-work."

She saw the look, the one that said he wasn't impressed. And was he just a little bit jealous? "My uncle's offered me a job at the Radford," he said suddenly. "What d'you think?"

Jess didn't know what to think. Kyle's uncle was a surgeon. Kyle was a clever young man but he didn't have those sorts of skills. "As what?"

"Patient liaison. He reckons I've got the right touch — you know, good with people, able to put them at their ease. It was me that suggested it." He grinned. "A place like the Radford should have someone who's on the patient's side."

"Would you like that sort of work?"

"Well, it's better than what I'm doing now. Working in that insurance office is dead-end stuff and I want something with a future. My uncle Clive has the major financial stake in the Radford Clinic, hence its name, and he'll see me right. He's promised me a good salary and prospects. No medical experience required."

Jess wasn't sure. It sounded all right, but it wouldn't do for her. Everything she'd got in life she'd worked for. She'd always made her own way without recourse to family favours. "What sort of surgeon is he, your uncle?"

"Heart mostly. He fixes arteries, you know, fits stents and does bypass surgery. He's hoping to open a new renal unit. A doctor he's recently met wants to invest money in the Radford and run it. He wants to carry out transplants and the like." He laughed.

Jess shot him a look. "That's not funny, Kyle. Someone has had to die to make a kidney available."

"Calm down. I know it's no joke, but it is what he does. I know it's serious stuff, that's why it needs some lightening up."

"D'you think you'll take him up on his offer of a job?" Jess asked.

"Nothing to lose, have I? He wants me to start next week. A fortnight's induction followed by a course in Manchester, and I'm in."

Jess nodded and poured another glass of wine. "So, you're going to ditch the humdrum insurance job. Well, don't forget your old friends, will you, after you become a high-flyer."

"No chance of that. I certainly won't forget you," he said, and there was a twinkle in his eye.

* * *

When Harry got back to the station, the incident room was empty. However, there were several uniformed officers in the room next door, and he could hear their chat and laughter. He checked the time, gone eight in the evening. He'd work a bit longer and then go home. He stared at the incident board and gave a cheerless smile. Home. That wasn't how he thought of Ryebridge. It was okay but it was nothing like where he'd come from. In that moment, Harry realised how much he missed his hometown of Dunoon and the familiar faces. It was the first time he'd really felt the wrench of missing it, and it hurt. The feeling had crept up on him almost without his noticing, and he knew it would tear at his heartstrings until he did something about it.

But for now he had work to do. No time for wallowing in nostalgia. Anyway, there was no way he could return, not if he wanted to stay alive. Harry shook himself and put his momentary self-pity down to tiredness. He picked up the marker pen and wrote the name *Paula Rushton* on the board. She was young, living her life, and he had a bad feeling about what might have happened to her. The boyfriend had texted him the photo, so he printed it out and pinned it next to that of Lori Lansing. He'd no evidence to back it up but he considered the notion of a serial killer. But when he saw the images of the two women side by side like this on the board, he was immediately struck by how alike they were. Same size, same short dark hair, both looking as if they could do with a decent square meal.

His mind was playing tricks, had to be. Harry was tired. He told himself to shelve this stuff until the morning. But he couldn't leave it alone. He pushed back a stray lock of fair hair from his eyes and looked again at the board. He was missing something. A piece of this puzzle that would make everything fall into place. He had the victims' names but what he didn't have was a motive for either Lori's murder or Paula's disappearance. He yawned and swore. He'd been up since first light and was too tired to work things out. All he could do for now was keep everything crossed, hoping that Paula hadn't ended up like Lori. And then there was the clothing. Paula had taken it to the launderette, so how come Lori ended up wearing it? Had it been stolen? Had Paula been forced to give it to someone? Whatever was the case, why would anyone want to dress a murder victim in such a way?

Harry flopped down on the nearest chair. He was weary and his head hurt. Despite all the new bits of information they'd been getting, sorting this case was getting no easier.

Col burst in through the incident room door. "You look done in."

"The nature of the job." Harry yawned. "What's got into you? You're far too energetic for this time of day."

"That's because I might have something." Col grinned. "We had a call earlier from a woman called Mrs Porter, who lives in a semi overlooking the park. She's seen the reports in the papers about the murder and reckons she saw something."

Harry's head shot up. "And did she?"

"She's an early riser, and that morning she recalls seeing a dark blue van on the track that runs through the park. She noticed it because it wasn't from the council and she thought perhaps the driver had strayed into the park by mistake. The driver parked up for several minutes and she began to suspect he was there to dump rubbish. She was all set to tackle him, went outside for a better look and to tear the driver off a strip, but he drove off before she got the chance." Col gave Harry a nod. "There was nothing written on the side of the van but she noted down the registration number."

At last, something they could use. "Check it out," Harry said. "Let's see what we get."

Col sat at his computer for several minutes. Finally, he looked up. "You'll never guess who the registered keeper is."

Harry was too tired for guessing games. "Just tell me what you've got."

"The van is registered to Blackwood's club, the Rainbow."

Bingo! At last this was something solid they could use against Blackwood. "We need another word with the man before we finish for the day. Get uniform organised to pick up that vehicle."

CHAPTER TWENTY-ONE

Jess sipped on her wine and gave a nod of appreciation. Kyle had said that tonight was on him and had ordered the most expensive bottle of red in the place. "Very nice, expensive though. I thought you were watching the pennies — that apartment you've got your eye on, remember? You can't rent forever."

"Doesn't matter now I've taken that job with my uncle Clive. He's given me an advance and he assures me that now I'm working with him, my money worries are over."

Jess was curious and just a little jealous. "Which side of your family is he from?"

"My mum's. He's her adopted brother. My grandparents took him in when he was ten. I don't know the full story, but apparently he had a dreadful time of it when he was a little lad. Social services stepped in, and eventually he became a member of our family."

"That was good of your grandparents. A child of ten can be tricky. It's not like taking on an infant."

Kyle nodded. "They didn't want Mum to be an only child. After Granny had Mum that was it, she couldn't have any more. Then, as soon as she saw Clive, she fell in love with him."

"He was a lucky boy."

Kyle had hold of the menu. "Fancy a pudding?"

She smiled. "I couldn't eat another thing. That steak was more than plenty. Anyway, I might not stay awake long enough to eat it."

"Surely I'm not that boring. Am I?"

"It's not you, Kyle, it's the job."

"I'll have to have a word with that DI of yours."

Jess smiled. "He's okay. Harry is a good sort, and there are plenty in the force who aren't. No, it's this case that's wearing me out, it's wearing Harry out too. We're struggling if I'm honest, and there's still no sign of a breakthrough."

Suddenly Kyle's mobile rang. Jess shook her head but he ignored her admonition.

He looked at his watch. "Uncle Clive? What's up? Is it important?"

Kyle held the phone away from his ear, his uncle ranted on so loudly that Jess could hear every word. There was some problem with a disgruntled patient's family. Even though Kyle hadn't officially started yet, it was obvious that he'd be expected to be at his uncle's beck and call day and night. He'd certainly earn that wage he'd been promised.

"An angry customer," Kyle explained once the call was finished. "Clive wants me to go over, calm things down."

"I was under the impression that you hadn't been taken on yet, that you were still making up your mind. I know you want the job and the money's good, but don't let him bully you, Kyle."

"It's not like that," he said.

But it had sounded just like that to Jess. Clive Radford had really been shrieking at Kyle. He wanted him at the clinic and no excuses. At this rate, his young nephew would have no life of his own.

"Uncle Clive is under a lot of stress at the moment. I need to make sure he's okay."

Jess grabbed her things ready to leave with Kyle. She'd get a taxi outside the Rainbow and have an early night.

* * *

The evening was still in its infancy as far as clubbing was concerned, and the Rainbow was quiet. The atmosphere was no different though. Half an hour after Jess had left, Harry and Col went in through the main doors and made for the bar, where they asked for Blackwood.

The barman scrutinised Harry's badge. "Sorry, mate, you're out of luck. The boss is away for the night. It's his wedding anniversary and he's taken the lovely Carla somewhere special to celebrate."

"Do you know where?" Harry asked.

The man laughed. "No, but even if I did it'd be more than my job's worth to tell you. Mr Blackwood would skin me alive. He's due back tomorrow morning, you can see him then."

Frustrating as it was, it looked like there wasn't much choice.

"Can I help?" someone asked from behind them.

It was David Parsons, the manager, and Jess's old schoolfriend.

"We're looking for Blackwood," Harry said. "It's important, but perhaps you can give us the information we're after. The club owns a small blue van. Who has access to it?"

Parsons smiled. "We have two small dark blue vans, Inspector. They are identical, apart from the registration numbers, and all the staff are allowed to drive them. We use them for picking up stock."

"Where are they now?"

"Safely garaged at the side of this building. Why d'you ask?"

"One of them was seen by a witness at the place where the body of Lori Lansing was left," Harry told him. His nerves were badly frayed. He looked around and saw they were getting the usual interest from the security men standing at the bar. The last thing he wanted was trouble from them. "I'm afraid I'll have to impound them," he said quietly. "Our forensic people will need to examine them both."

David Parsons didn't argue. He went round to the other side of the bar and took two sets of keys from under the counter. "This unlocks the garages, and you have a set of keys there for each van. Kindly bring them back once you're done."

He hadn't turned a hair, he had complied at once, with no argument. Not what Harry had expected. David Parsons, at least, wasn't trying to hide anything. "Be sure to tell Mr Blackwood when you see him, and that we'll return them just as soon as we've finished."

"You've only just missed Jess," David Parsons told him. "Her and her friend left early. I do hope there's nothing amiss."

The man was fishing. Harry smiled. "I wouldn't know. But they're both busy people."

CHAPTER TWENTY-TWO

Thursday

Despite being dog-tired the evening before, Harry had still managed to pack his belongings for the move. He wanted to leave Ryan's on Thursday morning and go straight to Jess's after work. The boot of his car was full of suitcases, the back seat piled high with still more, plus boxes stuffed with his worldly belongings. Was this all his life amounted to? It wasn't a lot to show for the years. A sober thought and it unsettled him. Jess was right, he needed to sort himself out, make a decision about his future. Was it to be a career here in the north of England, or should he return home to Dunoon? He knew what he'd prefer, but was it feasible? Could he really return home and pick up where he'd left off? The sad truth was: unlikely. Too much had happened, there'd been too many changes to simply pick up the threads, and then there was the continuing threat to his life. No way could he live comfortably in a place where Mungo Salton was likely to find him. The man wanted revenge, wanted his blood for an imagined wrong. There was nothing Harry could do to put the man right, so it was better to stay out of his way.

Jess might be a work partner but she was also a real friend for taking him in again. He knew she didn't want him there. He thought her tidiness verged on the fanatical, but it was her house. This time he'd be sure to watch his step, live by her rules not his. Upsetting her a second time round was not in the plan.

Harry had rung Jess first thing and brought her up to speed regarding the vans belonging to Blackwood's club, and the missing girl, Paula Rushton. They met in the car park at the station and Harry got into her car. "I had the two vans brought in last night and they're with Forensics. Some of Hettie's people are dealing with them while the rest are turning over Paula Rushton's flat." He looked at Jess. "We need to find that girl. Something is very wrong there. While we deal with Blackwood, I've got Col looking at the missing person report her boyfriend filed."

"I do recall seeing Paula's name on the list when we were trying to find out who Lori was," she told him. "I noticed she was local but there was no suspicion of foul play. Most people who disappear don't need help, we mustn't forget that."

Harry shook his head. "I've got a horrible feeling that this particular young woman does need our help, Jessie, and it might already be too late."

"Are we bringing Blackwood in then?" Jess asked.

"We'll speak to him at the club first and I'm hoping that things don't get tricky. Initially we want answers to a few questions about those vans. We leave the real pressure until we see what Hettie finds. She gets evidence that Lori was in one of those vans and Blackwood's feet won't touch. He knows something, and the vans are only the start. He's behind most of what's wrong in this town right now. We mustn't forget that, and we mustn't forget his wife Carla either. She knows Paula too, so we'll speak to her later."

The pair were about to pull out of the car park and make for Blackwood's club when they saw his sports car pulling in. Blackwood, looking perfectly relaxed, got out and walked towards them with another man in tow.

"Graham Hollis, my solicitor," he said. "I'm told you've confiscated my vans and that you want a word."

As smooth as ever, not so much as a ruffled feather.

"Thanks for coming in," Harry said evenly. "You'd no need to trouble yourself, we would have come to you."

"No problem. We were passing," Blackwood said.

"This shouldn't take long." Harry led the way to an interview room on the ground floor. "You've no doubt been told that our forensic people are looking at your vans. The search is just routine at the moment. I simply want to rule them in or out of our enquiries. You see, one of them was spotted by a member of the public at the very same time and place Lori Lansing's body was left."

Neither man looked particularly perturbed by his words. Blackwood said, "How dreadful. Surely you can't think that I or any of my people had anything to do with that?"

"The truth is, I don't know what to think. Your van was at the scene, Mr Blackwood, and I cannot ignore that," Harry said.

"We're looking for any trace of Lori's DNA," Jess warned him.

"You won't find any," Blackwood said. "Lori did come to my club but as far as I'm aware, she never had any reason to ride in one of our vans." He paused for a moment. "However, I will ask my employees, every last one of them, to make absolutely sure."

"Have you finished with my client?" Hollis asked.

"One last thing," Harry said. "Did you ever meet a young woman called Paula Rushton?"

Harry watched as Blackwood thought about this. He had to admit that the man didn't look startled at the mention of the name. "No, I don't think so," he said. "But then, so many people come to the club. I talk to a lot of them, Inspector, so I wouldn't want to swear to it."

"Your wife knew her."

Blackwood rolled his eyes. "Don't tell me. Another lost cause from that bloody theatre group of hers."

"How did you know that?" Jess asked.

"For six months of the year that group are the only people Carla bothers with. Ryebridge theatre is her life."

"You referred to Paula as a 'lost cause'. Why?" Harry asked.

"Let me guess. This Paula is young, probably has no job and comes from that damned estate, the Baxendale."

Harry nodded.

"Carla tries to involve the community, particularly the young folk she sees as no hopers. Believe it or not, she came from there herself and is keen to give something back."

"Very laudable." Though Harry wasn't really impressed. He'd reserve judgement about Carla Blackwood until he'd spoken to her himself. He stood up. "Right, that's enough for now. Thank you for coming in. When the forensic checks are done, we may have to speak to you again."

Blackwood and his solicitor left, as relaxed as when they'd come in.

"What d'you think?" Harry asked.

"Blackwood was far too casual for my liking. I have a sneaky feeling that he has something up his sleeve, and that even if Hettie does find Lori's DNA, he'll have some plausible explanation for us to chew over."

Harry agreed with her. Blackwood was as slippery as an eel.

CHAPTER TWENTY-THREE

As if Gabby French didn't have enough to worry about, her brother, Dillon, still hadn't returned home. The problem with Dillon was that he had a foul mouth and was prone to use his fists at the slightest provocation. Though where she and Ollie were concerned, he was always kind-hearted and tried hard. Aware of the threats from the landlord, Jack Leyburn, he'd left two days ago to get some help with their housing predicament. Gabby feared that he'd tackled both Leyburn and Blackwood and come off worse. For all she knew, he could be lying in some back alley with his head bashed in.

Her front window was still barricaded up. She and Arthur were the last two left on the terrace, and either Leyburn or Blackwood's thugs could return at any time. Then what? The lone constable standing out there on the pavement would be no match for them.

A woman from Social Services had taken old Mrs Hardy away, promising to do something about sorting a place for Gabby. Gabby wasn't holding her breath. She'd been here before and was used to the wait, the promises that came to nothing. Reluctant as she was to leave the house empty, she had to do something about Dillon. What choice did she have?

Gabby dressed Ollie in his warmest clothes, put him in his pram and went to have a word with the nice detective who'd come to their rescue yesterday. He needed to know about Dillon being missing and her fears for him.

* * *

"Telling Blackwood we wanted a word with his wife might not have been the brightest thing to do," Jess said, as they made their way to the theatre.

"If he warns her and she tries to avoid us, so what?" Harry said. "We'll pick her up and then she'll have to explain what she's so afraid of. Blackwood is the key to this case, I know it. Despite what he says, he knew Lori, and Carla knew Paula. There is a connection somewhere."

The theatre was busy when the detectives arrived, they were doing a read-through. The players on stage were in costume, and Carla Blackwood was directing operations. They heard her bark out orders, her local accent booming around the hall.

"Looks a bit flushed. She's not happy," Jess whispered.

Harry looked at the long face. "She doesn't look like someone who'd be happy at much. I'd like to be a fly on the wall when her and Blackwood are at home together."

"What d'you want?" Carla shouted. "Deliveries are at the rear of the building."

Harry held up his badge. "We're not delivering anything, we're police," he called. "We need a word, Mrs Blackwood."

Carla Blackwood was tall and willowy with mid-length blonde hair. She'd aged well, like her husband. With ill grace, she gave the people on stage a break and came over to join them, her face a picture of displeasure. "Is this about Paula?"

"Yes, the girl has been missing for several weeks now and her boyfriend is concerned."

That brought a smile to her face. "Are you sure he even notices, Inspector? The boy is off his head on cocaine most days."

Harry didn't like her attitude. "Oh, he's noticed all right, and he was coherent enough when he spoke to us."

"Look, it's all very simple. Paula and I had words over a mug of coffee that got spilled. I admit I may have been a little harsh, but Paula is clumsy. The drink went all down the front of the costume she was wearing. I snapped at her but soon calmed down. I told her to get it dry-cleaned and gave her the money to do it." She stood with her arms folded. "That was it. There's not a lot more I can tell you. She left here with the clothes in a bag, heading for the shopping precinct over there where there's a dry cleaners and launderette."

"Didn't you worry when she didn't get back to you?" Jess asked.

"No, I realised what an idiot I'd been to give her the cash in the first place. I'll lay odds it went straight into the pocket of that boyfriend of hers and he'll have sniffed it up his nose. Paula will have been too embarrassed to come back to the group."

"And the costume?" Jess asked.

"I know what happened to it." Carla looked uncomfortable. "Anna told me about you finding Lori's body dressed in it. I have no explanation for that and can only presume that whoever Paula passed the clothing to was responsible. But Lori and Paula were friends. Lori was wardrobe mistress at that time, so she had a valid interest in what happened to the costume. She was upset when Paula spilled the coffee down it."

"Didn't you think to report Paula missing when she didn't return to the group?" Harry asked.

"No, it's not my place. The girl has that boyfriend, and probably other people who know her better than I do."

"It appears that no one has heard from Paula for some time. We need to have a word with her about what happened to Lori." Harry handed Carla a card. "If Paula contacts you, you ring me at once."

They were about to leave when Anna Noble, red-faced and flustered, came rushing across and handed Carla a mobile. "It's happened," she gasped. "What we were afraid of."

Harry saw the fear in Carla's eyes as she took the phone. She listened intently and then said, "I'll come right away." She turned back to the detectives. "Sorry, I've got to go. I'm needed elsewhere."

"Nothing too serious, I hope," Jess said.

"So do I, but I'll just have to wait and see."

Harry nodded to the door. Time to go.

CHAPTER TWENTY-FOUR

"She's been waiting a while." The desk sergeant nodded to a young woman seated on one of the benches. It was Gabby French.

She looked drawn and tired. Harry wasn't surprised, life on Victoria Terrace must be hell. He knew that Jess had made numerous phone calls on Gabby's behalf but was still waiting for positive news, so he had nothing good to tell her.

"The kid's a bit fractious," the desk sergeant said irritably. "Been yelling his head off."

Harry could see that Gabby was doing her best to keep him quiet. She was bouncing the infant on her knee and making soothing noises.

She looked up when Harry approached. "He's teething."

"Are you okay, Gabby? Nothing else has happened, I hope," he said.

"My brother Dillon still hasn't come home and he hasn't been in touch. He does stay with his mates sometimes but not without telling me. Mostly he dosses at mine with me and Ollie." Her eyes, wide and anxious, searched Harry's face. "Something's not right. I have no proof, just a gut feeling. Me and Dillon are close, he's in trouble I just know it. D'you understand what I mean?"

Harry did indeed, he trusted his own instincts. "Where was he going when he left you?"

"To see Leyburn and Blackwood. He wanted to persuade them to back off for a while. As you saw for yourself yesterday, it didn't work. After that performance on the street, I expected him home, but there's been no sign of him."

"I take it he has a mobile?" Harry said.

"Yes, but he's not picking up. I'll text you his number. D'you think you might be able to trace him from it?"

"We can give it a go. Text me a photo of him too," Harry said.

Jess came into the reception area and joined them. "Has anyone contacted you about accommodation?"

"No, and I doubt they will, to be honest," Gabby said. "I've been here before. The social housing people always promise the earth but they deliver nothing."

"I've rung a couple of housing associations," Jess said. "I'll ring again, remind them how urgent it is."

Harry looked at the skinny girl and pale sickly-looking infant and understood Jess's need to do something.

Jess squeezed her arm. "I'll be in touch, don't worry."

"We'll do our best to find Dillon. We'll keep you informed," Harry added.

"You can't imagine how worried I am. You get anything on him, let me know at once," Gabby said. "This waiting and not knowing is doing my head in."

"I feel for her," Jess said, as soon as they were alone. "Apart from her brother and the baby, Gabby's got no one and she's so young."

Harry felt the same but what they could do was limited. Harry couldn't even find anywhere to live himself and had to rely on the kindness of friends. "There are dozens like her, Jess. We can't fix the lives of all of them."

Back in the incident room, Harry added Dillon French's name to the board. "He's missing," he told the others. "He was going after Blackwood and Leyburn for hounding his sister. I just hope to God he turns up safe and well." He wrote

Dillon's mobile number on the board. "Get a list of his calls over the last couple of weeks and find out when the phone was last used. Ask Sasha to triangulate a position for that last call too." Sasha Steele, Professor Hector Steele's daughter, was in charge of communications and data.

Col was on the office phone. Call finished, he turned to the others. "Terry Blackwood has been carted off to the Radford. Apparently, he collapsed at the club, but we've no idea why. I did ask the bloke who volunteered the information but he doesn't have a clue. All he knew was that one of the Radford's fancy ambulances came for him."

Harry was surprised. They'd had no idea the man was even ill. You'd never guess it to look at him. "That'll be what the phone call Carla got was about," he said to Jess. "And why she had to leave in such a hurry."

"I'd really like to know what ails him. Is there any way we can find out?" she asked.

"The doctors won't tell us, Jess," Harry said. "You know what they're like. They'll just fling all that patient confidentiality stuff at us."

"When I think about it, I could see she was upset, but I got the impression she wasn't surprised at the news. And didn't that woman, Anna, say they were expecting it?"

"He's collapsed before," Bob Tait said from the back of the room. "I was with my father-in-law at some golf club do about a year ago. Blackwood became more and more sick as the night went on. At first, folk thought he'd drunk too much, but then down he went. He was hospitalised for a week, after which he appeared to be back to normal."

Interesting as this was, it still didn't tell them what was wrong with him. Harry's instincts were at it again. Illogical as it was, he couldn't rid himself of the idea that Blackwood's condition was important to the case.

Col changed the subject. "I've dug out the letters and photos sent to Lansing. I went through them but there's nothing that helps. I've made copies and left them on your desk."

Harry nodded. "Thanks, I'll look over them shortly." He turned to Bob Tait. "Have a casual word with your father-in-law, see if he knows anything more about Blackwood's illness. Anything he can tell us could be useful."

"I could ask Debra," Jess suggested. "She'll have seen and heard lots of things while she was working at the club."

"Good idea," Harry said. "Speaking of Debra, has Hettie been on with anything from that alley where she was attacked?"

"Her team's collected bags full of rubbish — cigarette ends, empty soft drinks cans and chewing gum, the lot. They're working their way through it, to see if they can pick up any DNA belonging to people we're interested in. We have the names of Blackwood's security team, and all but one have records, so their DNA is on the system," Jess said.

"The one with no record. Is there anything of interest there?"

"He's currently off work with a broken femur, which he got after a fall three weeks ago, so the manager says," Jess told him.

"Unlikely to be involved in that case. Anything on either of Blackwood's vans, or Paula Rushton's flat?" Harry asked.

"They're still hard at it, and as Hettie's pointed out, her team is spread a little thin. She said not to expect anything fast," Col said.

"Is Debra still in hospital?" Harry asked.

"No, Harry, the constable watching her reported that she was back in her flat, recuperating," Jess said.

"It might be an idea for you to pay Debra a visit shortly," Harry told Jess. "She spends a lot of time behind that bar at the club and must be privy to all sorts of gossip."

Harry stared at the board. First Lori, then Paula and now Dillon French. All three had just disappeared into thin air and they still didn't know why. He could only hope that Paula and Dillon wouldn't end up like Lori.

* * *

Adam Lansing was in limbo. The police had told him little or nothing about the investigation into Lori's death. They hadn't even allowed him to see her body, and that hurt. What he wanted more than anything else was an end to this, a funeral, after which he could make an attempt at a new start. He'd never get over the loss of Lori, but he had the rest of his life to get on with.

Friends advised him to get on with work, it would help take his mind off things. But it didn't. Work had become boring and meaningless, he couldn't bring himself to care how the supermarkets he owned were doing, they were not where he wanted to be. Only now that Lori was gone had it hit home how much she'd meant to him. As for the money he earned, what was it for?

He stood staring out of his front window, looking at the distant street, watching everyday folk doing everyday things. They were lucky. He, on the other hand, was lost, daydreaming about a life in another time, a time when he'd been one of the happiest men alive. All he wanted was for things to be that way again. Little did he know that in a few seconds, he would be offered the opportunity to do just that.

His reverie was interrupted by a sudden loud ringing. The phone. He hoped it was the police with news, but it was something far greater.

"There's still time to get her back." The magic words. "You'd like that, wouldn't you, Adam? To have Lori with you, have your life back, the two of you living happily together like it used to be."

His first thought was that this was some chancer trying to extort money, some heartless rogue who'd read about the case in the papers. But it couldn't be, the voice sounded right, exactly like the previous time. He was even using the same gruff whisper to disguise it.

"You're . . . you're lying," he stuttered. "My Lori is dead."

"You're wrong. Your Lori is very much alive and wants to come home. I can arrange that, Adam, and soon, but it'll cost you."

Adam had been here before and lost a fortune. "I don't believe you. Besides, I have nothing left."

"You own a lot of property. Sell something, raise the cash. You know people in this town who'll be happy to make a deal."

That was true. Jack Leyburn wanted the land his Ryebridge supermarket and its adjoining car park was built on. He'd promised him a good price too, said he had cash waiting.

"I can't simply take your word for it. The police found a body. They've done tests and they're sure it's Lori."

"They're wrong."

Was he telling the truth? If he was, Lansing daren't pass up the opportunity. "I'll need positive proof that Lori is alive and that the woman in the morgue isn't her."

"And you will get it, Adam. The body the police found was not Lori. Do we have a deal? I give you proof that Lori's alive, you give me the money I ask for. Not as much as last time. I'll settle for two hundred thousand. Sort the cash and I will return her to you. But be warned, go to the police and this time she really will die. I promise you that."

He had no choice. More than anything, Adam Lansing wanted his wife back. "Okay," he said slowly. "We have a deal."

CHAPTER TWENTY-FIVE

Debra lived in a flat above a newsagents off Ryebridge High Street. The entrance to it was off a small yard around the back. Jess banged on the locked door and looked up at the window above. The curtains were closed. It looked like no one was at home.

Jess took out her mobile and gave Debra a ring. "It's me outside. I won't keep you, I just need a quick word."

It took Debra a good five minutes to get down the stairs. "I'm as stiff as a board. Every joint aches and so does my head, then there's my arm. I can't do anything properly with this plaster on and it'll be weeks before it comes off. Doesn't matter what I shove down my throat, nothing touches the pain."

Jess had to admit that she looked a state. Her face was still badly bruised and her eyes were swollen. "I'm sorry," she said. "You took quite a beating."

"And it shouldn't have happened. This is down to you lot, and then you have the cheek to come back. What is it now?"

Jess completely understood Debra's anger. She was right, it was their fault, but that couldn't stop them turning to her for help when they needed to.

"Blackwood has been taken ill," Jess said. "He's in hospital."

The news didn't appear to come as a surprise. Debra simply nodded and led the way up to her flat. "It'll be his old trouble. He gets like this. It'll pass, and then he'll be back to his usual self."

The flat was small, a combined living room and kitchen plus bedroom and bathroom. It was untidy, Debra's stuff lay strewn all over the place.

"I can't tidy up, the pain's too bad," she said, sitting amid the heap of rubbish on the sofa. "The best I can manage is to sit here and watch the box all day."

"D'you rent this off Leyburn?" Jess asked.

"What choice do I have? There's bugger all else out there. That man has the monopoly on crap accommodation in this town. He charges the earth for it too."

Jess hadn't the time to get into a protracted discussion about Leyburn's evil ways, so she returned to the subject of Blackwood. "You said it would be Blackwood's old trouble. What exactly did you mean?"

Debra shrugged. "I don't really know what it is. Some sort of illness that puts him in hospital now and then. He's never said anything about it and I've never asked. None of the other staff know owt either, cos we've discussed it. He has regular appointments at that private clinic, but I've no idea why. Treatment or check-ups of some sort, I suppose."

"You sure you don't know, Debra? You called it his 'old trouble', as if you did."

"I just meant that whatever it is he's had it for a while. He's secretive about it. I reckon the only person who really knows what's wrong with him is that wife of his — oh, and I reckon Lori knew. Despite what folk will tell you, they were close. Before she disappeared, they spent a lot of time whispering together at the club. Lori was always very attentive, made sure he took his meds, that sort of thing."

"You think Blackwood really liked Lori?"

"Yes, I do, but she was always wary when Carla was on the prowl. I reckon they pretended otherwise to stop the gossip, not that it worked."

"Could he have killed her?" Jess asked.

Debra shook her head. "He had a soft spot for Lori. If she'd made a nuisance of herself, I reckon he'd have found another way to deal with her."

"This 'old trouble', Debra. Do you have any theories about what it could have been?"

"No, love. No one ever said owt and I didn't pry where I wasn't wanted."

Jess was disappointed, though she knew Debra wasn't holding out on her, that wasn't her style. "Thanks. I'll leave you in peace. Sorry again for what happened. If I could make things different, I would."

"They came to see me, you know, when I got out of hospital — Blackwood and his wife." She nodded at a bunch of roses in a vase. "They brought me them and a huge box of chocs."

Jess wasn't impressed. "Payment for having you done over."

Debra shook her head. "I've changed my mind about that. It was the way he was, things he said. I got to think-ing and I don't reckon what happened to me was down to Blackwood at all."

Jess could barely believe what she was hearing. Of course Blackwood was responsible, who else was there? "He might not have carried out the attack himself but he'll have been behind it. Because if it wasn't him, Debra, who could it have been?"

"I don't know, but a girl gets an instinct about these things. He's been so good to me, kept my job open and is still paying me full wages while I recover. Why do that if he had me beaten up in the first place? It doesn't make sense."

"It could be down to guilt," Jess suggested.

"An alien concept to Blackwood, love. Sympathy, yes. Guilt, never. Anyway, you've got no evidence, so if it's all the same to you, I intend to forget all about it and get on with my life."

She was right about the evidence, they had nothing except the badge Debra had yanked off whoever was responsible. What they needed now was Hettie to come up with proof she could wave in front of Blackwood's face before charging him.

Back in her car, Jess rang the lab. "Hettie, I'm sorry to press you but we really do need a break with the case. Have you got anything at all of any use?"

"The rubbish from that alleyway gave us nothing," Hettie began. "But we're working on Paula Rushton's place now and we've found several items of interest. One of them being an amount of cocaine."

"We've met her boyfriend and he looks every inch the user. I'm not sure if he lived with her or not, but chances are he'd have access to the place. Anything else?"

"Yes, and this is the confusing bit. I've run DNA tests against several items we took away and have come up with a match."

"Noel Tomkins?" Jess asked, assuming it would be Paula's boyfriend.

"Yes, but there is plenty of DNA from someone else too. One Jamie Wilson, a small-time dealer from Salford. He's done time, hence his DNA is on the database. There's also a third person's DNA, but as yet we have no match for that."

Wilson. The name had come up before, but she didn't think he was local. "He's new to Ryebridge in that case. Perhaps he's involved with the dealing Paula's boyfriend was into. He could well be the one supplying Tomkins."

"It's not as simple as that," Hettie said. "There is something else, which I find extremely puzzling. You'll find it as hard to get your head around as I did."

Was there nothing simple about this case? "Just spit it out, Hettie," Jess urged.

"Wilson's DNA is also a match to the foetus Lori was carrying."

Jess's eyes widened. She wasn't just puzzled, she was downright shocked. Everyone thought Lori was in a relationship with Blackwood, so what was going on? "You're telling me that he's the father of Lori's unborn child? This Wilson? How can that be? We had no idea she even knew him. And what was Lori Lansing doing associating with a lowlife drug dealer like him anyway? She wasn't a user. I might have understood it if she had been."

"No matter how unlikely, DNA doesn't lie, Jess. I'll email you the report and you can read it for yourself."

CHAPTER TWENTY-SIX

Harry couldn't get his head around Hettie's findings any more than Jess. "I want Wilson finding and brought in. Get uniform on it. We must have some information about his usual haunts on record. Check out the lot of them. That young man has questions to answer."

"Have you considered that he might have killed both Paula and Lori?" Jess said.

"It has to be a possibility," Harry said.

"I've found Wilson's record on the system, sir," Bob Tait called out.

Harry went over to Bob's desk to have a look. He gave a thin smile. "Lori, Paula, Tomkins and Wilson. What were the four of them up to? We know Paula and Lori knew each other, but where do the others fit in?"

"Tomkins thought he was in danger of losing Paula to Wilson, but he must have had something going with Lori too. What d'you think?" Jess asked.

Harry was looking at the incident board. "I'm not sure what to think right now. We have to accept that despite her and Wilson being an unlikely match, we must have got it wrong." They stood looking at the board in silence, reflecting. "What d'you see?" Harry asked Jess after a while.

She shrugged. "Notes, charts and faces. What're you getting at?"

"This case has been niggling me from the start, and when I saw the photo of Paula Rushton, it niggled me even more."

"Go on. Where's this come from? You didn't discuss any niggles with me."

"I needed something more before I said anything," he admitted. "What puzzled me most was why go to all the trouble of obliterating Lori's face but leave that tattoo on her arm with her name on it if the intention was to make her unrecognisable?"

"I didn't think of that," Jess said, realising he had a point. "You are a dark horse, Lennox. You should have said something. We could have thrashed it out together."

"We didn't even know about Paula then. Until we had more information, I had nothing to base my theory on."

"Well, we have now so come on then, let's hear it," she said, plonking herself on the nearest chair.

"What if the body found in the park isn't Lori Lansing?" he began. "What if it was Paula Rushton who was murdered and not Lori?"

Jess thought for a moment. "I can drive a bus and anything else you like through that one. We have Lori's DNA from her toothbrush, and it matches what Melanie got from the body lying in her morgue."

It was hard to argue with that, except . . . was it the correct DNA? "We had a sample that was got from a toothbrush that we *believe* belonged to Lori. But what if it didn't? What if that toothbrush was taken from the Lansing home and switched with one belonging to Paula?" He looked round at the team, who were hanging onto his every word. "Which one of you collected the toothbrush from Adam Lansing?"

The team looked at each other and there was a lot of muttering, but no one admitted to getting that toothbrush. As Harry suspected, the person who had gone to the Lansing house and done the pickup was not one of his team.

"If I'm right, I suspect that the toothbrush handed in at the Reid was not Lori's."

"We can speak to Adam Lansing again," Jess suggested, "ask if he can describe the man who collected it. That apart, you know what this means?"

"Yes. Hettie told us that she'd received the DNA and simply accepted it. We should have asked her who took it there, and when."

"To be fair, the sample might simply have been left at reception with her name on it. There is CCTV at the Reid. We can look at the relevant footage," Jess said. "What I don't understand is why? Why kill Paula and make out that the victim is Lori?"

"Half a million quid," Harry said simply. "Perhaps Lori planned it all herself, or perhaps she had help from Wilson, but I suspect she wanted to leave her husband and decided to fleece him first."

"It's a bit extreme. Why not just get a divorce?"

"Perhaps she realised she'd never get that much money by simply divorcing him. Lansing is in business, a lot of what comes into his shops comes in cash. For all we know he could have money stashed away, and Lori didn't reckon much to her chances of getting her hands on it. Or she might have known that a half share of their combined assets wouldn't give her that much either."

"What about the breakfast? After the autopsy you checked that with the husband, and he remembered what she ate. Paula must have eaten exactly the same as Lori that morning."

Harry shrugged. "If Paula was being held and Lori was in on it, it would have been easy enough to arrange."

"If you're right, and I'm not saying you are," she cautioned, "we're a long way off proving it. What you're describing takes a lot of planning. Whoever did this went to a great deal of trouble."

"They were doing their best not to get caught, Jess. Don't forget, the rewards were high. Lori gets the lion's share of her husband's cash and the freedom to simply disappear."

"You're presuming that Lori planned this and that she isn't dead."

"Exactly, Jessie. I propose that we investigate the possibility and check the forensic evidence."

Harry clapped his hands to get the team's attention. "Finding Wilson and bringing him in is a priority. And while you're at it, keep your eyes peeled for Noel Tomkins and Dillon French. Both of them are users who will know Wilson." To Jess, he said, "You and me will visit Hettie, we'll pick up that CCTV footage ourselves, and then we'll speak to Lansing. We need to ask them both about the individual who picked up the toothbrush and delivered it to the Reid."

"It might be an idea to speak to the woman who runs that launderette on the Baxendale precinct as well. She must have been one of the last people to see Paula," Jess said.

"Right then, let's get to it."

Jess grabbed her things and the pair made for Harry's car.

"I did have that word with Debra by the way," Jess told him, "but she wasn't much help with Blackwood's illness. All I found out was that whatever his condition is, he's had it awhile and receives regular treatment. And get this, she now doubts it was Blackwood who had her done over." Jess shook her head. "She stood there, black and blue with bruises, showing me the flowers he'd bought her. So now he's Mr Wonderful and can do no wrong."

"Perhaps he's paid her off," Harry said. "Could Blackwood be worried that we might actually have evidence against him? We do have that badge, remember."

"She said she knew instinctively it wasn't him. Was quite firm about it."

"Instinct, eh. Well, I can understand that. Mine's been in an uproar for a couple of days now."

Jess rolled her eyes. "You manage to successfully go with your instincts often enough. I suppose Debra and Gabby could both be right? How d'you want to play this? Hettie first, or Lansing?"

"Hettie. We'll ask her to check the body's DNA against any of Paula's they've found in her flat. Then we'll look at the footage and see if we can get a half reasonable image to show to Lansing. We'll visit the shopping precinct on the way back."

"If we're right, then it's likely that Lori isn't dead, which means she never was pregnant," Jess said.

Harry nodded. "Makes sense."

"So Lori could still have been having that affair with Blackwood. Paula's death, making the body appear to be hers, could be part of a plan for them to do a runner together."

Harry considered Jess's theory. If she was right, she'd just put Blackwood back in the frame. "Blackwood has a successful business — granted, not all of it's legitimate, but he makes a lot of money. Carla has been with him a long time. Why give up everything for Lori?"

"Perhaps he loves her. Love makes people do odd things. Debra is convinced that Lori was a big feature in Blackwood's life, she says there was definitely something between them."

"For now, we'll keep it in mind." It was all Harry would commit to.

"What d'you think has happened to Dillon?" Jess asked.

"Nothing, I hope. The last thing we need is another dead body on our hands."

CHAPTER TWENTY-SEVEN

The pair arrived at the Reid and went straight to Hettie's office. Harry was hoping that she'd understand his concerns about the body and be able to help them.

"I've had Col on the phone," she said. "He told me that what you suspect has happened, and the body we thought was Lori Lansing is really this Paula Rushton woman." She smiled grimly. "It's a weird one, even for you. Anyway, we'll soon know if it's true. I'll do tests against some of the items collected from Paula's flat and see if there's a match with samples taken from one of those vans.

"The toothbrush first. It was delivered here by a man I took to be one of your uniformed officers," Hettie went on. "I didn't think to question it. We'd spoken about it and I was in a rush, I was just coming in from being out on a job when he caught me. He handed over the evidence bag, said you'd told me all about it — which you had — and that was that."

"Did you recognise him?" Jess asked.

"No. I didn't take much notice, being more interested in the evidence. He wasn't one of the officers I know, and I've met most of them. I took the item straight to the lab and got on with the processing."

"Would you recognise him if you saw him again?" Jess asked.

"Probably not. It was all so fleeting."

Jess nodded. Like she said, it was the evidence that was more important.

"CCTV?" Harry asked.

Hettie handed him a micro disk. "There's not much to see and it's more back of the head than full-face stuff, I'm afraid. He must have been aware of the camera in reception and did his best to avoid looking at it."

Just their luck. Nonetheless, they'd give it a go. "None of my team picked up that toothbrush from Adam Lansing," Harry told Hettie. "You'd said we should get something of Lori's but I hadn't been specific enough when telling my lot."

"All is not lost," Hettie said reassuringly. "I can do two things straight off. The evidence bag for a start. I'll test it for prints and DNA, see what turns up. If he wasn't wearing gloves, we might get something and you never know, the man might be known to us. Plus we now have some results from the flat and like I said, we also have results from the two vans belonging to Blackwood. I can extract DNA from various samples we got from one van, namely blood and hair, against that of the body. There was no shortage of material. The back of both vans is carpeted and in one of them we got nothing but in the other, the carpet was covered in bloodstains. I think that's where our victim was beaten following the surgery. That strongly suggests to me that it was that particular van the body was moved in."

"I now think that was Paula Rushton not Lori," Harry told her. "But we still have no idea where Lori is. I may be wrong, but I think she's still alive."

Hettie listened to the pair intently. "An elaborate scam if you're correct, but if you are, we have all the evidence to prove it. I'll do the relevant tests as a matter of urgency, and then, perhaps, we'll be able give your body her real name."

"What about the tattoo?" Jess asked. "If Harry's theory is correct, Paula must have had one identical to Lori's."

Harry realised Jess had just made a vital point. It had been important in the initial identification, as Lansing had recognised it.

"I intend to have another look at that too," Hettie said. "Anything suspicious and I'll get back straight away."

"Got anything yet on the football club badge?" Jess asked, keeping her fingers crossed. "Sorry to keep on, but I really want the bastard who attacked Debra."

"DNA yes, but no match I'm afraid. Here's something for you, though. We found the same DNA on the door leading into the kitchen in Paula Rushton's flat as that on the driver's side of the van the body was moved in. I'll give whoever he is credit, he'd worked hard at leaving no trace, but he'd forgotten he'd moved the sun visor with his bare hand, and I got the tiniest trace of sweat."

Harry realised this meant that whoever had attacked Debra must have known Paula and had access to that van. As far as they were aware, the only connection was the Blackwoods. Terry knew Debra, and Carla knew Paula from the theatre group. He looked at Jess, who nodded. "You know what I'm thinking, don't you? That pair gets everywhere."

"If the same DNA turns up anywhere else, let me know immediately," Harry told Hettie.

"I will but with no match on the database, I'm not sure it'll help. The one certainty is that it doesn't belong to anyone currently involved in the case. We have DNA profiles from Blackwood, his minions and Adam Lansing, so it's none of them, I'm afraid."

Harry's concentration had wandered. He was thinking about Jamie Wilson, and if he could be their killer, but his DNA was on record too. This case got no easier. He'd no sooner decided that one of them was the culprit, than he was forced to realise he had the wrong man.

CHAPTER TWENTY-EIGHT

Jamie Wilson was worried sick. The police were all over the estate, knocking on doors and asking about him. He needed to do a runner, first back to Salford and then further afield until things cooled down. Trouble was, he needed money to do that. He'd left his stash of cocaine in the flat. By now the police would have been all over it with a fine-toothed comb, so they'd doubtless found it by now. No drugs meant no chance of earning a few bob off his regulars. The only avenue left to him now was to demand the money he was owed by the man he'd been working for.

He was holed up in the Dog and Gun on the edge of the Baxendale, hoping that Ray, the landlord, would help him out with a few quid. But Ray was adamant. "No way, Jamie. Apart from not being able to afford it, I've been bankrolling you these last few weeks and it's already cost me a fortune. Enough is enough. From now on, you're on your own."

"Please, Ray, I'll pay you back. I'm owed plenty, the lying bastard I've been working for just needs to pay me."

"Blackwood? Idiot, you should know better than to get involved with him. You'll have to go and ask him, son, cos you're getting nowt from me."

"I never said it was Blackwood," Wilson insisted.

"He's the moneylender around here, so you didn't have to." Ray poured Wilson a pint and pointed to a table in the corner. "Get over there, keep your head down and don't cause any trouble. Make your calls, sort what you're owed, then get the hell out of here."

If only it was that simple. The man he'd just finished the job for, and who owed Wilson, was a dangerous piece of work. He'd proved that with what had happened to Paula.

From his vantage point by the small window, Wilson could see the uniformed coppers going from flat to flat along each of the decks of the tower block. How long before they cast their net wider and found him? He looked at Ray and weighed up his chances of snatching the cash from the till. But he was the only person in the pub, and he knew that Ray always banked the takings from the day before first thing, so no easy money there.

Wilson had no choice but to make that phone call.

"Your boss owes me," Wilson said to the man who answered. "I've waited long enough. I need the money quick. The police are chasing me, so I need to get lost for a while."

"It's not that simple. You've been a stupid boy, Jamie. You cocked up. I've heard the police have been to that cow's flat and that they've got the vans. You know what that means, don't you? They'll find your DNA all over it and come looking."

"That's why I need the cash. You said you'd pay when it was done. I've sorted my part, now you have to pay up like you agreed."

"We've already had the police here. The boss'll go mad if he finds out. I'm not taking any risks right now, you'll have to wait."

"You can't go back on our deal now. Tell your boss I've said nowt to the police." Wilson was angry, the man was holding out on him. "I can see the police now, they're on the estate. All I have to do is shout and they'll take me in. I'll spill my guts, I promise you, I'll tell them everything. Better you just pay up while you can."

"Not a good idea, Jamie, and a dangerous move. The boss can finish you with a click of his fingers."

A cold shiver ran through Wilson's body. The man wasn't joking. His boss wielded a lot of power in this town.

"Your best plan, Jamie, is to do a runner. Go back to Salford and look for help there. I have no intention of giving you anything, so do yourself a favour and get lost."

The man finished the call, leaving Wilson angry, confused and afraid. His first impulse was to find him right now, teach him a lesson he wouldn't forget. He'd show the bastard that cheating him out of what he was owed wouldn't work, that there'd be consequences. Trouble was, he'd come off worst.

Ray picked up Wilson's empty beer glass from the table. He had a grin on his face. "Going to cough up, is he? I don't know who you're dealing with, lad, but if it has anything to do with Blackwood, you haven't a chance in hell. Which is a shame, cos I could do with getting back some of what you owe me."

Wilson stared at him. "We're both out of luck. The bastard won't pay and there's nothing I can do to make him."

"Like I said, one powerful man. Still, even powerful men have their weaknesses. Threaten him, tell him you'll put the frighteners on his family. Even Blackwood can't ignore that one."

Wilson nodded. It was a plan of sorts. "I have to do something. I'm going to get my own back if it's the last thing I do."

"Be careful, lad. Ryebridge has its share of villains who won't hesitate to stick the knife in, and Blackwood is the worst of the lot."

"I never said it was Blackwood."

Ray plonked the empty glass on the bar with a laugh. "You don't have to. I've lived in this town long enough to know how things work."

Jamie Wilson got to his feet and kicked out at the chair he'd been sitting on. "Thanks for nothing, Ray. I won't be sorry to see the back of this bloody place, or you."

He walked out into the gloom of the late afternoon, pulled the hood of his jacket his face and sneaked round the back of the pub. Jamie had a mate who ran a betting shop a few doors down from the Rainbow club. He owed him and would let him wait in the back room out of harm's way until darkness fell.

The sooner he got shot of this town the better. He'd get his money and disappear. There were people he knew in Salford who could get him out of the country until everything cooled down. No way was he taking the rap for Paula's murder. Not when he was innocent.

CHAPTER TWENTY-NINE

After Hettie, Adam Lansing was next on the list. Jess had rung ahead to tell him they were coming and he was waiting for them expectantly.

"You've got news for me?" he asked.

Harry glanced at Jess and shook his head. He felt a great deal of sympathy for the man. If his theory was correct, Lansing had been hoodwinked in the most cruel way.

"We're investigating several lines of enquiry," Jess said.

"I know the jargon, I've heard it all these last few weeks. That's what you people always say when you're getting nowhere fast."

"Things are moving on, sir." Jess said. "We're after some more information, if you're up to it."

He sighed. "Ask away."

"The officer who came here and picked up Lori's toothbrush, did you speak to him?" she asked.

"No. I didn't actually meet him. I had to go into Manchester for a meeting with my suppliers that day. I arranged with the officer who called me to collect the toothbrush from my supermarket in Ryebridge, where I'd left it with my manager. He said the officer picked it up at about ten that morning."

"D'you have CCTV in the store?" Harry asked.

"Yes, but only over the tills, not the entrance. We have so little pilfering we didn't think the expense was necessary. It was agreed that when he arrived he'd ask at the help counter and my manager would hand it over, which he duly did. There was nothing untoward about it, otherwise I'd have been told. Everyone who knows me is aware how important the case is to me."

Harry knew what this meant. Whoever had picked up the toothbrush knew enough about the Ryebridge store to realise he could get in and out without leaving a trace on film.

"There's nothing wrong, is there?" Lansing asked anxiously.

Jess gave him a smile. "We're simply checking one or two details."

"Details, details, that's all you lot talk about," he said angrily. "When are you going to arrest someone for my wife's murder?"

"We're getting close."

The lack of conviction in Harry's voice obviously wasn't lost on Lansing. "Look, I'll help all I can, but I need you to move on this. I can't even organise her funeral because the morgue won't release her body until you say so."

There was no way they could tell him that the body in the morgue was unlikely to be his wife. That they believed she'd done a runner with both his money and whoever she was having an affair with. Currently, the odds were in favour of that being Blackwood.

"Thanks," Harry said. "We'll talk again."

The pair hurried back to the car. "If your theory is right, Harry, he'll be devastated. The poor man has no idea what has been going on."

"We can't help that, Jessie. When we find out the truth, he'll have to be told. If Hettie proves me right, we're going to pull out all the stops to find Lori Lansing. She's part of this and she's as guilty as sin. It won't go down well with her husband, but he's just going to have to accept it."

* * *

They knew, Adam Lansing realised. The body language and the tone of voice spoke volumes. But why hadn't they been honest, told him the truth about the evidence they'd got? More importantly, how had they found out that Lori wasn't dead, and how would it affect the deal he'd struck with her kidnapper?

Lansing pressed the return key on his laptop and watched the footage again. Lori smiled and waved at him from the small screen. He was pleased to see she looked well, unharmed. But she did ask him to help her. She said she was missing him and wanted to come home. Behind her was a television with that morning's news playing, the proof he needed that the kidnapper had not lied. His Lori was indeed very much alive.

Lansing had spoken to Leyburn and brokered a deal that suited them both. Solicitors for both parties were drawing up documents and Lansing would have his money within days. Leyburn would take both the Ryebridge supermarket and the large car park adjoining it. In a few months, he would flatten the lot and put up houses. The locals would have to shop elsewhere.

* * *

"The Baxendale shopping precinct next?" Jess asked. "A word with whoever runs the launderette and then back to mine. I saw your car when you pulled in for work this morning and you've a lot of unpacking to do. Before the day is done, I want you to find a place for every single item. And you make sure you abide by house rules. I don't want to find your smelly socks behind every cushion."

Despite the attitude, Jess was a good sort. She'd taken him in when he had nowhere else to go. He wouldn't forget that.

The launderette was open until seven. A woman called Nora Pritchard was at the counter most days. She eyed the pair up and down when they entered and rested the mop she'd been holding against the wall. She sniffed. "You're police. I'd know you lot anywhere. You here about Paula then?"

"Yes," Jess said. "We'd like to know about the last time you saw her."

"Why, what's the stupid girl gone and done now? I know something's happened cos she's not been in 'ere in weeks, and as a rule she's in most days. That theatre company treated her like a skivvy, they 'ad her running round getting stuff washed and ironed from dawn till dusk."

"She helped look after the costumes," Jess told her.

"I know, but that wasn't really her job. She and that other one were always fighting over who would wash the stuff next. Paula was thrilled to bits when they finally gave her a part in a play. I don't know what happened for sure but that last time she came in 'ere in tears. She'd 'ad a falling out with her mate when some coffee got spilt on her frock." Nora smiled. "It were one of them frilly, old-fashioned things, a bugger to iron. I told her as much too. She should have had it dry-cleaned like she were told, but no, that cost too much. I got the impression she'd already spent the money, so she just bunged it in one of the machines and hoped for the best."

"Her mate, the young woman who helped her with the costumes, d'you know her name?" Harry asked.

"They weren't really mates, it was Paula. She was obsessed with her. She was a posh piece from the other side of town. It were Lori this and Lori that. Whoever this bloody Lori was she'd got Paula well under 'er thumb. I only got a look at her the once. Paula, the stupid girl, had her hair cut and done in the same style as her, and she only went and got a tattoo just like Lori's. I mean, why do that? She paid good money for it too. I asked and she said Lori wasn't bothered. Paula reckoned it would make them friends for life. She was wrong on that score. The ink were hardly dry and they were at each other's throats. Once she started with the dieting, I told Paula to call it day. But would she listen? Would she 'ell. Lori was stick thin so that's what Paula wanted too. Hardly ate a bite these last weeks, silly lass."

138

"What did they argue about?" Jess asked.

"They went around together for a while. The theatre for one, but they went to that club in town too. Paula would never say what it was but they were arguing about something all right. The last time I saw Paula were a few weeks back, and she weren't well. I thought it were the diet but she had a pregnancy test kit in her pocket. It fell out when she were looking for coins for the machine. I asked her about it — if she were pregnant like. She said to keep me nose out and that it were for a friend. Not that I believed her. She had that look about her, sickly and worried."

"Are you sure you don't know what they argued about?" Jess said.

The woman folded her arms and glanced around her, as if to make sure no one else was listening. "I reckon Paula were thinking about a termination and Lori were against it. Not that they told me anything, but I could read between the lines. There was raised voices and the word 'hospital' was mentioned."

This was interesting but it didn't fit with what they knew. The pair thought the two women had locked horns over a man.

"Where to now?" Jess asked as they left the dry cleaners. "I don't know about you, but I think we should call it a day."

"Got a date?"

"Kyle's taking me to the Rainbow again. Despite the atmosphere, he actually likes the place."

"I'd like to check the Radford, make sure Blackwood is actually there and if he is, why." Harry checked his watch. It was getting late and he should get back and unpack. Blackwood could wait until tomorrow. "Okay, we'll call it a day. You drop me at the station and I'll update the board and pick up my car."

"You've got your own room back and there's some extra cupboard space in there now, so no mess. Got that?"

Indeed he had. He was grateful to have the room but knew he couldn't live like this for much longer. Sooner rather than later, he'd have to make a decision about his future.

139

CHAPTER THIRTY

Jess took hold of Kyle's hand as they entered the club. "I know you like it here but this place still gives me the jitters."

"I'll make a quick call and we can go somewhere else," he offered. A big smile lit up his face. "But I'd rather we didn't. I've got a little surprise for you."

Jess got a sudden sinking feeling. She didn't want anything heavy, just a relaxing night out with this interesting young man she was just getting to know.

"My uncle is joining us," he announced. "I've talked about little else but you all week, and he's dying to meet you."

Jess had no idea how to respond to that one. She was flattered, of course, but bemused and a little self-conscious. She tried to put the record straight, explain to Kyle that she wasn't really that exciting. "I'm a sergeant in CID, Kyle. It's nothing special. I work hard and with the right breaks I might make DI before long."

"Don't do yourself down. You work on all the big cases around here. You and that Scottish bloke are well thought of."

She grinned. "Wait till I tell him. Harry'll be made up. On second thoughts, his head's big enough as it is."

As they crossed the room, Jess glanced over at the crowd round the bar and spotted Debra. She had a drink in her hand and appeared to be enjoying herself. Couldn't keep away from the place, obviously.

Kyle led them to a table, summoned the waiter and ordered a bottle of wine. "We won't order our food yet," he told the man. "We're waiting for Mr Radford to join us."

He'd kept that one a secret. Jess gave him a look that plainly said she wasn't happy. "He's a busy man, your uncle. Running that hospital, carrying out all those operations, I'm surprised he's got the time or energy for a night out. You should have told me. I thought it was just the two of us this evening."

Kyle looked embarrassed. "When I told him I was bringing you here, he asked if he could join us. He's interested in who I see, likes to keep an eye on me, that's all. As for having the energy, he's still young enough to stand the pace. You're right though, the Radford is getting busier by the week. I wonder sometimes how he fits it all in. He's got the usual run-of-the-mill stuff, and now on top of that he's got his special patients to see to."

"Special patients? I thought they were all special. They pay enough for their treatment."

"Yes of course, but my uncle is a first-class cardiac surgeon. Recently he's been taking on more patients with heart problems. The Radford now has a ward and operating theatre designated solely for their treatment."

"Isn't that all stents and stuff?" she asked.

"I don't know the ins and outs, Jess, I'm not at all medical, but I do know he plans to expand. He's about to take on a partner who's a renal surgeon. All's sorted for him to start at the end of this week. Apparently, he'll be able to offer new treatments and is already getting startling results."

She nodded. "That's kidneys. But that's all dialysis and pills. Once that fails to do the trick, all that's left is a transplant."

"I'm not sure, but people come in as an emergency and several weeks later leave happy and healthy."

Jess was puzzled. That wasn't what she understood to be the outcome for someone with serious kidney problems. In the end it boiled down to a transplant or death. She'd be interested to know what Clive Radford's secret was.

Kyle nudged her. "Here he is now."

Jess looked up to see a middle-aged man with greying hair and a slight paunch making his way towards them. He pulled out a chair and sat down.

"This is my uncle Clive," Kyle said.

Clive Radford greeted her with a smile. "Now Kyle's employer too. And you must be the lovely Jess, one of the brave detectives protecting this town."

He was smooth enough, she'd give him that. Gone was all trace of the enraged despot she'd heard bellowing at Kyle down the phone. "Detective, yes. Brave, I'm not so sure." Jess smiled. "Nice to finally meet you. Kyle often talks about you."

"To slag me off most likely." He chuckled. "But I understand, it's tricky taking up a new position when you're not exactly sure what it is you're supposed to be doing, and with a relative too. He's a long way from Cornwall and that old job of his, and the money's a lot better."

"I'm sure Kyle will do his best," she said.

"All he has to do for now is learn how the Radford works and fit in. Keeping his nose out of things that don't concern him will help."

Jess couldn't work out what Clive meant by that. She smiled. "Been snooping, Kyle? Having a nosey at the patient records?"

Clive Radford must have decided he'd said enough as he made no comment, and Kyle looked decidedly nervous.

"You certainly treat all the local bigwigs. You've got Terry Blackwood with you currently, I hear." Jess was hoping Clive might let something slip, but no chance. No one was more surprised than she at his response.

"You must have got your information mixed up, Jess. True, Terry is an occasional patient but we haven't seen him in months."

Time to change tack. This was something to think about later. "Kyle tells me you're a heart specialist and you're getting great results with the treatments you offer. Have you approached the NHS, told them what you've discovered?"

"Who's been telling you that?" he said. "It's just the same old treatment with one or two extras the NHS can't afford. Kyle is easily impressed." Was he just playing down his expertise? His answers were certainly evasive.

"He also tells me you're planning a renal unit," she went on.

"He has been talkative," Clive said evenly. "That's still in the planning stage. A renal unit will need financing, so I've deals to broker first."

Jess nodded as if she understood. Kyle had been far more positive about this renal unit than his uncle. He'd given her the impression that it was only a matter of time. What with that and his denial that Blackwood had been admitted, Jess was left wondering just what was going on.

Clive cleared his throat. "Right then, what are we having to eat? I'm told their steak and kidney pie is to die for, the trimmings too."

Jess nodded. "Okay, let's go with that then."

Clive Radford gestured for the waiter, who almost ran across. "We three will have the special," he said, "but give us ten minutes, my other guest is running a little late."

Kyle said nothing to this, so she presumed he must know who this other guest was. Radford's sudden appearance was surprise enough as far as she was concerned. Who else was about to appear? Jess had a bad feeling. There was something about Clive Radford that didn't ring true. He was pally with Blackwood, so he could be connected to anyone. Jess looked towards the doors, the place was busier than she'd seen it. People were pouring in, the tables swiftly filling up. Her attention was momentarily taken up by the waiter pouring the wine, so she didn't see the man approach their table.

"Sorry I'm late, unavoidable, I'm afraid. I've just struck a lucrative deal with Adam Lansing — you know, that supermarket bloke. I'm buying his Ryecroft site for my new estate. Got a good price too, the man's desperate for the cash. How the mighty have fallen." He laughed.

Radford leaned over and clapped his guest on the back. "Well done. Town centre site and all. Whatever you build there will fetch a pretty price."

Jess recognised the voice immediately. Jack Leyburn. Not a man she'd choose to dine with at any time, but more to the point, what was he doing with Kyle and his uncle?

CHAPTER THIRTY-ONE

"You must both know Jack," Radford said, "he's never out of the local paper." He clapped Leyburn on the back. "This is the man who's about to bring this town up to date. I've seen the redevelopment plans, once they're carried out, the renewal of the west part of the town will be the making of the place."

"Even more so now I've got my hands on the latest piece of land," his guest enthused.

Jess wasn't sure if Leyburn had recognised her or not. Their previous meeting had been fleeting but fraught. Time to take the initiative. "We meet again, Mr Leyburn." She watched for his response. For a few seconds he was puzzled and then his face fell as the penny dropped.

"You're one of those coppers who came to my office. One of the pair who put a stop to my men delivering eviction notices on Victoria Terrace."

"I'm afraid you've got that wrong," Jess said patiently. "What my DI and I put a stop to was a bunch of thugs getting heavy with innocent, vulnerable people."

"It's you that's got it wrong," he said, his face growing red. "That wasn't what was happening at all. The tenants all knew the score. They'd been given a date to be out of those properties and told that redevelopment was about to begin. I'm a businessman, I need to move on this quickly. I've men and suppliers waiting, and that all costs money."

"Were you there?" She watched his face fall. "Did you see those men, how they threatened a young woman with an infant in her arms with an axe?" She waited, but neither Leyburn nor Radford offered a response. "I witnessed the lot, the way those people were terrorised, and it was a flagrant breach of the law."

Jess got to her feet and grabbed her jacket and bag. "I'm sorry, Kyle, but I can't stay. This man features in our current investigation so it wouldn't be right."

"I won't tell if you don't," Radford said flippantly.

Jess looked at the surgeon as if he'd just crawled out from under a stone. "Not helpful." She turned to Leyburn. "Be warned. The matter of Victoria Terrace is far from over."

Jess had reached the main doors of the club when Kyle caught up with her and took hold of her arm. "Don't do this. Uncle Clive says he's sorry, he'd no idea what Leyburn had been up to."

"Sorry, Kyle, I'm no longer in the mood for either food or polite conversation. We'll speak tomorrow. Right now, I'm taking a taxi home." She kissed his cheek. "Get back in there," she said softly. "Your uncle will wonder where you are." He walked away, back to the table.

Her hand on the door, she heard a voice behind her. "Company not suit you?"

Jess swung round to see David Parsons. "It's a long story. Anyway, I'm tired. An early night will do no harm."

"You should get him to take you somewhere swish, somewhere in Manchester perhaps."

"It's hard enough getting the free time to come here, never mind travelling all the way into Manchester."

"Case proving difficult?"

Jess sighed. And some, but it was not something she could discuss with David Parsons. "The job in general, David, but we're getting there."

"It can't be easy, doing what you do. You'll be working on the murder of that woman I reckon, the one that used to come here."

"Sorry, I'm not at liberty to say." David was a pleasant enough bloke but his probing was making her nervous.

"Is there anything I can help you with?" he asked. "We've known each other a long time. I'd like to think that if there was anything you wanted to know about this place, you'd ask."

"Why, David, is this place or anyone who works here involved?"

"No, of course not, but these last few days you've hardly been out of here."

She shrugged. "Just how it is. I see the boss isn't here tonight," she said, chancing her luck that he might tell her something useful.

"Between you and me, Jess, the man's got problems on a number of fronts. In fact, I don't think Blackwood can keep all this going for much longer and I'm not just talking about his health issues. The vultures are gathering. It's got me worried, and others who work for him too. I know he's got a reputation as a villain, but this place and his other clubs are legit." He smiled. "The loan business is failing, though. Folk can't or won't repay, and the drug-running has all but been stolen from him."

Interesting as it was, Jess was tired and didn't pursue his comments. "His health issues? Is he ill then?"

"I'm not sure what's up with him, and neither is anyone else. But he's sick enough. He won't be back for a while, if at all. Meanwhile his businesses are vulnerable."

Jess would have asked more but just then, the security man, Edward, appeared. "Sorry to interrupt, sir, but you're wanted on the office phone."

"Sorry, Jess. I'll ring you. If you're free, perhaps we can meet up for coffee or something," David said.

Jess watched the two men disappear back inside, struck by Edward's behaviour towards David. He'd treated him like the boss, minded his manners and dropped the attitude.

* * *

Jamie Wilson made his way to the rear of the Rainbow, where the staff entrance was. Inside the hallway, he grabbed a passing waiter. "Boss in?"

"He's not well. You want something, speak to Parsons."

"Or you could always speak to me, son." The voice behind him had a broad Scottish accent.

Wilson spun round and looked at the man. He was tall, thick-set, and his face had seen a deal of wear and tear, so much so that his age was hard to guess. Wilson's eyes were drawn immediately to a long scar running the length of his right cheek.

The Scottish man obviously hadn't missed the look of distaste on the lad's face. He ran his index finger slowly down it. "The bloke who did this didn't live to tell the tale. There's no one here who wants to talk to you, so if I was you, I'd do one. We don't want any mishaps tonight, do we?"

Wilson had never seen the man before but it was evident from the wary looks of the security man who'd suddenly appeared that he carried a lot of clout. "Look, I've no argument with you, I just want what I'm owed. A word with the boss, he settles the debt and I'll be out of your hair."

"No can do," the Scottish man said. "I'd get gone while you're still in one piece and think yourself lucky."

Wilson was only a few steps away from the door that led to the bar area. From the noise, it must be packed. No way would the man or the guard try anything in public. "I'll see for myself, if it's all the same."

Before the stranger could make a move, Wilson was off, and seconds later was part of the crowd milling around the bar. "Lager," he barked at the waiter. "Is he in, I need a word?"

"No, love." Debra was at his side. "But I'd be careful if I were you, there're some strange types in tonight, folk I've not seen before. One of them, that rough Scottish bloke, is staying in the flat above."

No use to Wilson. All he wanted was his money for the work he'd done, and then he'd be happy to leave — the club and this town. He knew Debra worked here and, seeing the cast on her arm, understood why she was this side of the bar. "I'm owed," he told her. "The boss is holding out on me, and that wasn't part of the bargain. I'll pay you straight away is what he promised. D'you think the waiter would pay me out of the till?"

She laughed. "No way. Do that and Blackwood would skin the lot of us alive. Look, lad, do one before they throw you out."

Wilson was desperate. He was fast running out of choices. There was no money and no one here would help him. Perhaps a threat or two would bear fruit. He reached in the pocket of his hoodie and pulled out a knife. Grabbing Debra around the throat, he screamed for quiet, while he pulled the terrified woman towards the exit.

"Pay me what I'm owed," he screamed at the burly Scottish man walking towards him. "Pay me and I'll let her live!"

"Let the lady go, laddie," the man called out. "Do it now before someone gets hurt."

No way would Wilson do that. He had the upper hand now. They had no choice but to pay him. He wasn't sure about his next move, he'd work that out once he had the cash in his hands. Wilson expected them to back down, reach in the till and pay him. What he didn't expect was the sharp crack on the head. He fell to the floor, unconscious.

CHAPTER THIRTY-TWO

Friday

Something was wrong. Jess tossed and turned all night. In her restless sleep, something that had been said at the club the night before was working away at her mind, clamouring for attention.

The following morning she awoke with a start and at once realised what was troubling her. It was what Jack Leyburn had said about Lansing needing money.

Pulling a dressing gown around her slender body, she went to find Harry. She could hear him whistling downstairs, hopefully he had the kettle on.

"We need to talk," she said at once.

He grinned. "And good morning to you too. Don't snore that loud, do I?"

"No, idiot, it's about something I overheard last night in the Rainbow."

Harry had made a pot of tea and poured them both a mug. "I always knew that'd turn out to be a place of interest."

"Radford joined us, then Leyburn turned up at Radford's invitation. He was late. He'd been doing some deal with Lansing. He said that Lansing needed money and was selling him the Ryebridge store, which Leyburn was going to demolish and build houses on the land."

Harry considered this for a moment. "Lansing must be pretty broke. He did part with half a million, remember."

"Ryebridge is his flagship store. If he needs money so desperately, why not sell one of the others?"

"What're you getting at?" Harry asked.

"What if he's been pressurised for money again? What if he knows that Lori is still alive, been given proof perhaps?"

"Where would he get that idea from? We've let nothing slip," Harry said.

"I reckon he's been contacted again and asked for money. For him to want to raise the money so swiftly, he must have been convinced that Lori is still alive and is determined to get her back."

Harry nodded. "What d'you want to do? Tackle him about it?"

"It might be better to watch him and when he makes the drop, we pounce."

"That's not a bad idea, but how are we supposed to know when it's going to happen?" Harry asked.

"Check his phone records. He'll have been contacted by whoever is organising this. I'll lay odds it's not a number that usually rings him, and we can keep tabs on it."

"It's worth a try." Harry took hold of his mobile, rang Col and brought him up to speed. "Ask Sasha to check out all incoming and outgoing calls and tell her it's urgent."

"No probs. She's already been on about something else," Col said. "Says she'll catch up later."

"Having someone watching Lansing's house wouldn't go amiss either," Jess added.

Harry agreed. "If you're right, we might get a breakthrough on the Paula Rushton aspect of the case."

"There's another thing," she told him. "There's something odd going on both at the Radford Clinic and with Blackwood."

"Odd how?"

"I don't know yet. At the Radford it's something to do with private patients with heart and kidney problems. Clive Radford appears to have joined forces with a surgeon who has developed some new treatment that improves kidney patients' chances tremendously, not that I'm an expert."

Harry shrugged. "Clever man. I'm sure clinicians across the globe will be interested. And Blackwood?"

"Radford, who is Blackwood's consultant, told me last night that Blackwood is an occasional patient but he hasn't seen him for a while," she said. "But as we know from witnesses who were there when it happened, Blackwood collapsed at his club and was carted off to the clinic for treatment. So how come Clive Radford himself told me different?"

Harry looked at her across the table. "Are you sure about that?"

"That's what he said. Kyle and I were sitting with the man himself. Clive Radford is the boss, so presumably he knows who he's treating. Mind you, he's a shifty sod. There's something not right about him. He's not a man I'd like treating me, or mine."

"Couldn't you have steered the conversation, teased a little more out of both men?"

"I might have if we hadn't been joined by Leyburn. At that point, I'd had enough. Radford is one thing, but when Leyburn sat himself down at the table, I saw red and decided it was time to leave. No way could I sit there and make polite conversation with that creep. What he planned to do to those poor folk on Victoria Terrace was criminal."

Harry nodded understandingly. "Okay, let's find out for ourselves what's going on. Col will sift through Lansing's calls and I'll get him to have someone watch the house. You and me will pay a visit to the Radford Clinic. After that, we'll have another chat with Carla."

Jess agreed. "Odd though, don't you think? Why would Radford say he hasn't seen Blackwood? What has he to gain by that?"

Harry shrugged. "It is taking patient confidentiality to extremes. Perhaps he's being coy, on orders from Blackwood. The fewer people who know he's ill the more he can maintain his hold on his organisation. There are always villains waiting in the wings primed to take over, Jess. And Blackwood's empire would be quite a coup for whoever made a successful fist of it. Anyway, I'm curious about the place. I've never been inside the Radford. What d'you think?"

"Kyle won't like it. He'll think I'm either spying or out to cause trouble for him. Plus we can't just wander in there and ask to poke about, so what's our reason?"

"The need to speak to Blackwood urgently should do it," Harry said.

"If Clive Radford sticks to his story, we'll simply be told that he isn't there. What then?"

"We have what happened at the Rainbow for backup. The man collapsed in full view of everyone there. They can hardly deny that."

Harry was right. "Give me a couple of minutes to get my stuff."

* * *

The pair were only half a mile from the Radford when Harry's mobile rang. It was Sasha Steele from the Reid.

"Long time no speak," Sasha greeted him. "You were supposed to ring, remember, take me out for that drink."

"Sorry, Sash. We get this case sorted and you're on," he said.

His mobile was on loudspeaker and Jess heard every word. She turned, gave Harry a withering look and shook her head. No way would he keep to that one. For as long as she'd been working with him, women had been few and far between. She firmly believed he was still hankering after the woman who'd visited him from Scotland.

Personal stuff over, Sasha said, "I'm compiling a list of calls to both Lansing's landline and his mobile. I'll have it for you later this morning. Now, Dillon French. He made five calls from the Ryebridge area. Four of them pinged the mast in the park. But the last one was twenty-four hours ago from somewhere near the Radford Clinic. There's a mast right outside and Dillon's phone pinged it."

"Any idea who he rang?" Jess asked.

"No," she said. "All the calls were made to unregistered mobiles. That's the best I can do, I'm afraid. But I can tell you that his last conversation was over three minutes long. I'm still looking, so if I get anything else, I'll let you know."

"Thanks, Sash," Harry said, and finished the call.

"Why here? What's Dillon's connection to the Radford?" Jess asked.

"Could it be Terry Blackwood?" Harry asked. "He could have found out that he'd been taken there and come looking."

"Possibly, but when Dillon first went missing Blackwood hadn't fallen ill and was still working at his club. In fact, when Dillon left the house on Victoria Terrace, Leyburn wasn't really terrorising the residents. It was still in the realm of threats. He has to have gone to the Radford for some other reason, though I can't think of one straight off," Jess said.

"If there is a connection between Dillon and the Radford Clinic, we need to know what it is."

"I know. I'll ask Gabby," Jess said. "If she knows anything she'll be only too happy to help us. She's as anxious to find her brother as we are."

Gabby sounded much more positive. "I'm moving out. A mate has a squat near the college. She's going to let me and Ollie stay there for a bit."

Not ideal but probably safer than Victoria Terrace. "Are you still getting trouble from Leyburn's men?"

"A group of thugs came last night. They were shouting and drinking and at one point they set a fire in the middle of the street. Your copper rang for help and Leyburn's heavies did one, but they promised to return. I think I'm the last one left and I'm terrified."

Jess groaned inwardly. She had to do something for this girl. A squat was no place for her or the baby. She desperately needed somewhere safe and permanent to live. "I'll get back to you later today, I promise. I'll have a word with Leyburn too. Don't stress, Gabby, we are on your side."

"That's easy to say." Gabby suddenly sounded strained and sullen, like she had before. Gabby obviously doubted that she could do much to help, Jess realised. She didn't have much faith in her ability, and why should she? Jess had done little to help so far, despite all her promises.

"Does Dillon have any connection to the Radford Clinic? We believe he may have been there recently," Jess said.

"He'll have gone to see Blackwood," Gabby said. "He has treatment there."

"What business does your brother have with Blackwood?" Jess asked.

"Dillon was going to ask him for help, see if he could call Leyburn's dogs off. It was a last resort. Normally, he wouldn't waste his time but as you know, we're desperate."

"Why not just go and speak to Leyburn?" Jess asked.

"Blackwood has a lot of influence over him. Besides, Terry Blackwood is family."

"You mean you're related?" Jess hadn't seen that one coming. She could barely believe what she'd just heard. "In what way?"

"He's my dead mum's cousin. When they were growing up they were close. When Blackwood made it big, I expected him to help us, but I was wrong. Despite us being the only relatives he's got apart from his wife and kids, he doesn't want to know."

Jess didn't know what to say. She couldn't imagine anything worse than finding that you were kin to a man like Blackwood.

CHAPTER THIRTY-THREE

The pair left the car near the main entrance and went inside to the reception desk. Jess had the advantage of knowing Kyle and decided she'd use it. She flashed her badge at the receptionist, who looked flustered.

"We'd like to speak to Mr Kyle Stanton."

"I'm not sure where he is at the moment," the receptionist said. "Is it important?"

"It's regarding a patient of yours, Terry Blackwood," Jess said.

The receptionist wasn't just flustered, she now had panic written all over her face. "You must have that wrong. I don't think he's a patient with us."

"I think you'll find he is," Jess insisted. "Give whoever's looking after him a ring and tell him DI Harry Lennox and DS Jess Wilde would like a word."

The receptionist picked up the phone but her eyes never left the pair. Within minutes, Kyle walked towards them, looking ruffled.

"Jess. What is it? There's nothing wrong, is there?"

"This is official business," she said at once. "Serious too."

"If it's about the ruck in the Rainbow after you left, I assure you it had nothing to do with us."

Jess gave him a long hard look. She'd no idea what he was talking about. She'd have to make it her business to find out later. "We're actually looking for a young man called Dillon French. We believe he came here two days ago and he hasn't been seen since. We also believe his disappearance has something to do with Terry Blackwood, who is being treated here."

Kyle looked puzzled, his eyes darted from one of them to the other. "Dillon French, you say. I don't know the name. Are you sure about this?"

Jess nodded. "Perhaps you'd like to consult Mr Radford about that one. If Dillon is here, he's sure to know. Meanwhile, we'll have that quick chat with Blackwood."

"He definitely isn't here," Kyle assured them. "Or if he is, he's not down on our list of in-patients."

"Blackwood collapsed at the Rainbow yesterday and was brought here," Jess said.

"Look, I'll have to speak to Uncle Clive about this. Someone somewhere has got their wires crossed." He looked at the receptionist. "Check the patient register, see if Blackwood has been added to it today and let me know straight away."

Kyle showed the pair to an elegantly furnished waiting room and dashed off to find Radford.

"I reckon you're right, Jess. I get the distinct feeling that all is not well here," Harry whispered. "Could be because something nasty has happened to Dillon, and Radford is helping Blackwood to cover it up."

"He's got a lot to lose if that's what's happened. Better to tell the man to shove off and save both his reputation and the hospital."

Jess stifled a laugh. "I can't imagine anyone saying that to Blackwood, can you?"

They didn't have long to wait. Kyle soon returned, accompanied by Clive Radford. "There's obviously been some mistake," Radford began, a smile on his face. He turned to Jess. "It's like I told you last night, I haven't seen Blackwood for a while."

Jess gave him a look of disbelief. "He collapsed yesterday. He has some sort of health problem and you are his doctor. Where else would he go?"

Radford shook his head. "Well, you have me there. Perhaps he went to Ryebridge General."

"We were told that an ambulance from your clinic picked him up from his club," Harry said. "It was seen. If you wish, I can get the CCTV recording and show you. So it's pretty unlikely that he'd be taken anywhere else but here."

Radford's expression hardened, his usual suave self all but gone. "I'd advise you to leave well alone. You in particular, DI Lennox."

"We can't do that," Harry said. "And anyway, what's so special about me?"

"Persist and you'll find out," Radford said. "Look, I can't speak to you now. I'm busy. Some of the people I treat are seriously ill. I'm in the middle of a ward round and they need me. I can't ignore the needs of my patients, can I? After all, I am a doctor."

"You can't ignore the needs of those with money in their pockets," Jess said. "Like our mutual friend Blackwood."

Kyle waded in. "Look, my uncle's right. He's got things to do. I can answer any questions you may have."

Jess looked at him and shook her head. "It might be best if you leave this, Kyle. Your uncle has some serious explaining to do."

Radford nodded at Kyle. "She's right, son. I can answer for myself." He turned to the detectives. "I assure you Blackwood is no friend of mine. Moneylender he might be but he turned me down flat when I was desperate. After that, whatever relationship we had went out of the window."

"You were quite happy to eat at his place last night," Jess said. "But then you knew he wasn't there, didn't you?"

"Why did he refuse you?" Harry asked. "Surely he must have thought you and your clinic were a safe bet."

Radford shrugged. "He said he had his reasons."

158

"You surprise me. Blackwood knows a good deal when he sees one," Harry said.

Radford was fast losing his composure. "Look, I can't talk now, I'm expecting someone."

"I'm sure he'll wait. Why did Blackwood refuse to lend you money?"

Radford looked like a man who'd had enough. "He was warned off, Mr Lennox, by someone even he won't mess with."

Not something either Harry or Jess had considered. "What are you trying to say?" Harry asked. "Are you talking about some third party muscling in?"

"Leave it, that's my advice." Radford's voice was firm. He meant what he said.

"Okay, but tell me how ill is Blackwood?" Harry asked. "Men don't collapse for no reason, and it's not the first time either."

Radford glanced at the clock on the wall and shook his head. "You must leave, I couldn't help you even if I wanted to."

"But you told me Blackwood was a friend," Kyle said. "Now you tell me he isn't. I don't understand."

Jess saw that Radford was shaking. He kept looking round at the door leading to the corridor.

"You should consider telling us who you're scared of, Mr Radford, before your own health suffers," she said.

Radford said nothing for a while. "I have no intention of giving you any names but know this, there is a significant threat to me, Blackwood and anyone else who interferes with plans for this place."

"What plans?" Jess asked. "The new heart and renal departments?"

Radford looked at Kyle. "I told you to keep your mouth shut, son."

"This new venture, if Blackwood isn't investing in it, who is?" Harry asked.

"It's none of your business, and that's all I'm saying on the matter."

"I imagine it'll cost a fortune, so where is the money coming from?" Jess asked.

They had assumed that Radford and Blackwood were in cahoots, but apparently that wasn't so. Who, then, was the mysterious person who'd put up the cash. If it was purely a business transaction why not tell them the name of the investor? What was Radford hiding?

"You must leave now," Radford said. "The investor is only interested in making money and he doesn't care who he hurts in the process."

Kyle, who'd been standing by, hands in his trouser pockets, shook his head. "You should have said something, Uncle. I could have helped, spoken to him. He might have listened to me."

"Don't be stupid. No one can help. This is what happens to people who move in Blackwood's world. And as for Blackwood himself, his antics have attracted the wrong sort of attention from out of town."

If Radford wouldn't confide in them, there was nothing they could do. "If you change your mind and want to talk to us, Mr Radford, we can offer you protection," Jess said.

Radford gave a humourless laugh. "I am not going to talk to you, and you can't make me. As far as I'm aware, I've done nothing wrong, simply accepted a loan offered me by an associate. You see, I needed a small fortune to open and equip this place. The banks helped me up to a point but I was tens of thousands short. I was determined that this clinic would be the best, a centre of excellence. Currently we only take private patients, but eventually we would have taken some suitable ones off the NHS's hands."

"Basically, you're in hock to some stranger, and I'm guessing he now wants something in return and is threatening you if you don't pay up," Harry said.

"It's not quite as straightforward as that," Radford said. "We've managed to strike a deal that suits us both, so I'm hoping there'll be no more threats."

"Why is Blackwood here? You're not holding him against his will, are you?" Jess asked.

This made Radford laugh. "No. Okay, I admit he is here, but he doesn't want it made common knowledge. Blackwood is very ill. Make no mistake, the man will die if he doesn't receive treatment."

"Heart or kidneys?" Jess asked.

"You know I can't tell you that."

"If it is his kidneys and you've done all you can medically, from what I understand, that means a transplant. How d'you intend to manage that?" Jess asked.

The question hung in the air, while Radford seemed to struggle with what to reply. Finally, he said, "You're barking up the wrong tree, Sergeant. There is nothing wrong with Blackwood's kidneys."

"Okay, but while I'm here I'd like a word with him."

Radford heaved a sigh. "I'll get Kyle to take you to his room."

"While we're here, do you know a young man called Dillon French?" Harry asked.

"No, it's not a name I recognise. Why?"

"He's a relative of Blackwood's and he's missing. He came here looking for him and hasn't been seen since."

"What about Paula Rushton? That name mean anything?" said Jess.

Radford shook his head.

CHAPTER THIRTY-FOUR

Kyle led the way to a room at the far end of the corridor. "I wish I could help, Jess, but I've no idea what's going on here either. I'm as much in the dark as anybody."

Jess gave him a smile. It wasn't his fault his uncle was being protective. The less Kyle knew, the less involved he was in anything untoward. "When we arrived, you mentioned a ruck at the Rainbow after I left. What was that all about?"

"Some young bloke pulled a knife. He threatened that woman with the broken arm who works behind the bar. There was no harm done though. Some heavyweight strode in and sorted it."

Jess made a mental note to speak to Debra.

* * *

One look at the barrage of equipment Blackwood was hooked up to, along with the oxygen mask clamped to his face, and they knew expecting anything from him was a waste of time.

"Are you family?" his nurse whispered.

"Police," Harry said, showing her his badge.

"How ill is he?" Jess asked.

She shrugged. "Mr Radford will speak to you."

Moments later, Radford entered the room with another man and closed the door behind them. "This is Dr Kozlov. He's a specialist in renal surgery who's interested in buying a stake in the clinic. He's visiting today to get the feel of the place."

"Blackwood, what's up with him?" Harry asked.

"It's his heart," Radford said candidly. "Over the last five years he's had bypass surgery and stents fitted, but he's reached the stage that without a transplant he doesn't have long."

If that was right, it looked like whatever information Blackwood had, he would take it to the grave. Even so, Harry had to try. "Any chance you could give him something?" he asked Radford. "He may be the key to a murder we're investigating."

The nurse gave him an angry look. "That's not how we deal with our patients, Inspector. Villain he might be, but right now he's a patient in need of our care."

Everyone looked at Blackwood. The room was quiet, the only sound being the beep of the machines. All at once, Carla burst through the door, her face streaked with tears. She threw herself onto the bed. "You did this!" she flung at Harry and Jess. "You've killed him with your questions, your constant hounding. Murderers!"

"All your husband had to do was answer a few questions, deal with us honestly," Harry said. "I'm sorry it's come to this, but if there's any chance of him making his peace before . . . well, before the inevitable, I need to know what he says."

Carla stood up, hands on hips, and faced Harry. "My husband is not going to die. He's about to have a transplant and then he'll be fine."

That surprised Harry. For one, Blackwood didn't look strong enough and, secondly, where was the new heart to come from?

"Realistically, what chance is there of a transplant?" Harry said.

Carla glanced at the two doctors. "There certainly is, for the right price."

Harry took her to mean the cost of the surgery and the time spent here recuperating.

"Remember Paula's body and the missing kidneys," Jess whispered to Harry. "I've just had a scary thought. What if they were stolen for use here in this clinic?"

Paula had still had a heart though. Harry looked at Kozlov, the foreign surgeon Radford was showing around. Was his new role to be in transplant surgery? Paula's kidneys were missing as were the eyes and corneas, these organs were in short supply too. Harry felt a shiver run down his back. "Have you been told when a donor heart might become available?" he asked Carla.

"Today. Tomorrow at the latest," she said.

It was as he'd feared. "But transplants don't just happen like that. What about the donor? How can you be sure there will be one? There'll have to be a car crash or something for that to happen."

"Terry can't die," she screamed back at him. "He's far too young and he still has so much to give. He employs most of the folk in this town. What's the life of some young scally in comparison?"

Harry couldn't believe what he'd just heard. "What are you saying, Carla? You mean a donor has been found? D'you know who it is?"

"That no good relative of his from those slums by the canal. A perfect match, Radford says." Everyone in the room gazed at her in horror.

Harry turned to look at Radford, who was cowering by the door. The foreign surgeon was nowhere to be seen. "Is this true?"

"I had no choice," Radford said. "I refuse to do this and people will suffer."

It suddenly dawned on Harry that if they hadn't arrived when they did, Dillon would be dead by now. As far as he was concerned, Carla was totally wrong about her husband. Ryebridge would be much better off without Terry

Blackwood. "This stops now," he said bluntly. He nodded at Jess, who slipped off to call for backup.

"You are all coming down to the station," Harry told Radford, Kyle and Carla. "And if by some miracle he does pull through, Blackwood will be charged as well." He turned to Radford. "I want to know all about this neat little set-up. It also means you can no longer keep your investor's name a secret, I'm afraid."

"I'm saying nothing until my solicitor is present," Radford said.

Annoying, but Harry could hardly force the name out of him. He turned to Carla. "You knew about this and went along with the plan. You even knew who the victim was to be."

"I've done nothing wrong," she said sullenly. "I just want my husband back. All I know is that Radford has promised Terry a transplant. I didn't ask the details, nor do I care."

"Those *details* meant a young man's life. And you knew who the donor was to be. You said so."

"I don't care about that. I just wanted him back."

Harry had heard enough. Carla's attitude sickened him. "We'll talk again. There's still the question of what happened to Paula and Lori Lansing."

"Whatever happened to the both of them had nothing to do with me, or Terry," Carla said. "So you can look somewhere else for that."

"What happens now?" Kyle asked.

"You take me to Dillon. I want to make sure he's okay. Then you're coming to the station. We'll get a doctor to come and give Dillon the once over and have him transferred to Ryebridge General."

"Please, try to do this as quietly as possible," Radford asked. "We have many sick people here and they've paid good money for their treatment. And what about Blackwood? He's too ill to be moved."

"Once the doctor has seen to Dillon, he'll take a look at Blackwood," Harry said.

Kyle took his uncle's arm. "I'm coming to the station too. I'll arrange for your solicitor to meet us. He'll know what to do." He looked at Jess. "He was coerced, we all were, surely you can see that. What happened here was wrong, but Blackwood threatened him and his family, including me. Think on that."

"That's not our call to make," Harry said.

"Before we wrap this up, do the names Lori Lansing or Paula Rushton mean anything to you? I'm wondering if Carla was speaking the truth when she said they had nothing to do with them," Jess said to Radford.

He shook his head. "I know Adam Lansing from the golf club. Lori is his wife, I believe. Rumour has it she's left him."

CHAPTER THIRTY-FIVE

Harry had a shrewd idea that Carla was right and what had happened to those two young women was down to someone else entirely. Their problem now — how to find out who that was.

"I didn't have Radford down as a dodgy doctor," Jess said once they were back in the car. "Nor Kyle as his unwitting accomplice."

"Once he became aware that we knew what he was up to, at least Radford had the good grace to come clean and tell us what was happening. He didn't try to argue his case, he told us everything."

"And we got Dillon out. Gabby will be forever grateful," Jess added. "In fact, I'll give her a ring, tell her he's being transferred to Ryebridge General."

Harry drove to the station while Jess spoke to Gabby, who sounded over the moon.

"Two brilliant calls in one morning. You saved my brother and the council have given us a flat. A woman from the housing office came round and gave me the key this afternoon. I can't thank you enough, Jess. I must admit I was sceptical. I thought you would turn out to be like all the rest, but you're not."

Jess was flattered, until she reminded herself that she'd only done what anyone would who'd known about Gabby's predicament. "Dillon's in Ryebridge General. I'm sure you can visit, tell him the good news. Once he's on the mend, we'll get a statement from him. That is if he can recall what happened to him."

She finished the call and turned to Harry. "She's a good kid, she just needs a bit of luck for a change. The fresh start will do her good."

"Let's hope Dillon sees things like that too and gives up his habit."

Jess sat back in the passenger seat, going over what had happened. The outcome for Gabby was good, the only cloud on the horizon was Kyle. The notion that he was mixed up in this somewhere loomed large in her mind.

As if reading her thoughts, Harry said, "We need to know exactly where your boyfriend fits into all this."

Jess felt her stomach churn. She wanted to know that too and she didn't have a good feeling about it. "Kyle's a good sort, Harry. I'm sure he didn't realise what he was getting into. Talk to him, you'll see what I mean."

"How d'you know that? You know very little about him at all. It's not as if he's an old friend or someone from the town. And he was invited here by his uncle. Tell me, how did you two actually meet?"

"At a mutual friend's dinner party. She introduced me and we hit it off. There's no mystery there, Harry, so don't go inventing one."

"Did he get to know you before or after he knew you were a detective?" Harry asked.

"My friend Kate told him and he was intrigued. He asked me all about my colleagues and wanted to know how dangerous the job is."

Harry frowned. "Has he asked about your current case?"

"Of course not, and even if he had there's no way I'd discuss it with him."

"It's just that he's always around. He goes to the Rainbow, knows Blackwood and the Radford Clinic, and not content with that, he's wormed his way into your affections too. Surely you can see what I'm getting at?"

"There's hardly been the time for him to worm his way anywhere," Jess said. "We've known each other a matter of weeks, that's all. And as for always being around, he lives and works in the town, like me. And just because Radford was in Blackwood's pocket doesn't mean Kyle was too."

"Just be aware that we can't rule Kyle out of this, not yet. If we find he is involved, should we discover he knew Lori or Paula, I'd have no choice but to take you off the case."

That was the last thing Jess wanted. "He's got nothing to do with what's happened, I'm sure of it." She could barely believe what was happening. "If it makes you feel any better, I'll have another word with Debra, see if she recalls seeing him with Blackwood at the club. There's also whatever happened in the club last night to speak to her about. Pity I missed it. I'd have been very interested to get a look at this bloke who interceded."

Before Harry could reply, his mobile rang. It was Col, calling from the station. Harry put him on loudspeaker.

"We've got a problem, boss. Jamie Wilson has been found dead. A woman walking her dog in that wooded area in Ryebridge found him earlier this morning. I've alerted Melanie and she's got a team on it now."

Just what they needed. "Where exactly?"

"That piece of rough land between the lake and the swings. He's been shot in the head, sometime within the last twenty-four hours, Melanie reckons."

"You've had a good look round?" Harry asked.

"Yes. The photos have been taken and Forensics are on it. Hettie says he was dumped there, so we've no idea where he was killed. As you know, CCTV is a bit thin on the ground in the park but we'll do what we can."

Call over, Harry turned to Jess. "Wilson must have upset someone, but who?"

"That won't be difficult, given he's a dealer. But it must have been something serious for him to end up dead."

She was right. "Wilson knew Paula," Harry said, thinking aloud. "Someone as yet unknown wants us to believe that the body we found is Lori Lansing. We know too that Wilson was a dealer and probably supplied Paula's boyfriend and used their flat, but why kill him? What did he know or do that meant he had to be got rid of?"

"Perhaps whoever killed Paula did for him," Jess said. "That can't have been Kyle. He was out with me last night, I left him with his uncle and Leyburn and he's been at the Radford all morning, working."

She had a point. Had he been clutching at straws by suggesting Kyle Stanton was implicated somehow? Harry sighed. "Looks like it's going to be a long, hard weekend."

He took the next turn, which would take them through Ryebridge and into the park. He wanted to take a quick look at the scene and speak to Melanie. The park was close to the Baxendale, no place to linger at any time of the day.

"It looks like a professional hit to me," Melanie told the pair. "Grabbed around the neck — you can see the fingermarks on his right upper arm. Then, once the assailant had him on the ground, a single shot to the head. Quick, efficient and the work of an expert." She pointed to the part of Wilson's head that hadn't been blown away. "But there is also this. He was hit on the head prior to being shot. Not hard enough to kill him but he'd have been out of it for a while."

That gave Harry something to think about. Who did they have on their radar capable of carrying out a professional hit? Very few, that's for sure.

CHAPTER THIRTY-SIX

Harry told Col to get all the uniformed officers he could find out onto the streets. They were to go door to door around the houses bordering the park and on the Baxendale with a photo of Wilson and ask if anyone had seen him. They got nothing — that was until they asked at the Dog and Gun pub. Col rang Harry again and told him. It was the break they needed.

"The Dog and Gun pub, know it?" Harry asked Jess as they were pulling into the Baxendale.

"I'll say." She shuddered. "It's not somewhere I'd choose to drink."

"Well, Wilson spent yesterday afternoon there, so we need a word with the landlord, plus anyone else who was in there at the time."

For someone who ran a pub on the Baxendale, the landlord was surprisingly candid. Oh yes, he said, Wilson had been there.

"Terrified of his own shadow, the lad was. He made a few calls too. Reckoned someone owed him money and was refusing to pay." He nodded at the till. "Tried to tap me for a bob or two but I'm way past lending money to losers."

"Did he talk to anyone else?" Jess asked.

"No, we were the only two in here the entire time. He left it until dusk and then wandered off round the back. He didn't want to be seen by your lot, who were up in the tower block asking questions."

"D'you know where he was going?" Harry asked.

"He said Blackwood owed him. My guess is Jamie was making for that club of his."

"We can hardly ask Blackwood, given his condition," Jess whispered. "Anyway, he wasn't there yesterday, and as for doing a search, I doubt he kept financial records, not of his dodgy dealings."

"Records? That crook?" The landlord laughed. "I wouldn't waste your time. Now if you lot don't mind, I've answered all your questions and I'd like you to go. My regulars will be in any time. They catch me talking to coppers and I won't see them for dust."

He was right. He'd been honest with them and Harry appreciated that.

Back outside, he said to Jess. "First we need to know if Wilson actually went to the Rainbow. A word with Debra, I think."

She nodded. "We need a word with her about both Wilson and Kyle."

"The Kyle thing is bothering you, isn't it, Jessie?"

"Well, of course it is. We were doing fine and now this. I need to know if he's mixed up in what Radford's been doing."

Harry turned to Col, who was with them. "Get a statement off the landlord and then go back to the station, see if anything has come in from Sasha or Hettie."

"Sasha is still working on that list of calls for Lansing, reckons she'll ring you later."

Jess rang Debra's flat and was surprised that she picked up so quickly. She sounded much better.

"I'm off out to the club, love," she said. "Not working, you understand, just propping up the bar. Is this about all the excitement last night?"

"Partly. I was in last night, I saw you but I don't recall much excitement."

"It was after you left. That Wilson lad off the estate came in looking for trouble. He took on that friend of Blackwood's that's stopping in the flat upstairs."

So Wilson had gone to the Rainbow. Had he met with trouble and come off worst? But with no Blackwood calling the shots, who would have given the orders to get rid of him? "What happened?" Jess asked.

"That bastard Wilson only took a knife to my throat. I'm telling you, if that new bloke hadn't floored him, I'd have been a gonner."

So, Jess realised, this incident could indeed be the key to what had happened to Wilson. "We'll meet you at the club," she said. "Okay? Nothing heavy, just a chat."

* * *

Apart from Debra perched on a stool at the bar, the club was empty. Jess gave her a friendly wave and joined her.

"Where's your oppo?" Debra asked.

"He's anxious to know who's running the place while Blackwood is laid up. I left him round the back, knocking on the office door."

"Shame about Blackwood," Debra said. "Apparently it's his heart. I'd never have guessed. He keeps fit and tries hard at the diet stuff. Just goes to show, you never can tell."

"D'you mind telling me what happened last night?" Jess asked. "It is important or I wouldn't ask."

Debra gave her a long, hard look. "Summat happened? Is Wilson okay? He left here flanked by two of the new fella's people."

Jess shook her head. "No, he's not all right. The lad's been murdered, and we believe it has something to do with what happened in here last night."

"But it must have been an accident, surely? The lad was off his head, not fit to be out on his own. Anything could have happened to him. He kept going on about being owed money and needing to see Blackwood. He was angry, must have been, or he wouldn't have turned on me like he did. We'd been chatting at the bar, then suddenly he grabbed hold of me and pulled a knife." Debra's eyes widened. "I don't know about you, but having a knife held to your throat is no way to spend your time off."

"But someone stepped in, right?"

"Yes, some bloke I've never seen before. A proper hero he was, just my type too. Once things calmed down we got chatting. He's buying me dinner tonight." Debra grinned.

"Did this hero of yours take Wilson away?" Jess asked.

"He and some others dragged the lad outside but Scottie came back in. I don't know what happened then. A couple of hours went by and then the rest of them came back."

"You called him Scottie, Debra. D'you know his proper name?"

She shrugged. "I call him Scottie because that's what his people called him, and because of his accent."

"Where is he now?" Jess asked.

"Out, I think. Him and a mate are staying in the flat upstairs. Don't know how long for, though."

"Thanks, you've been an immense help. I'll get one of our constables to take a statement from you later."

Jess walked off and stood in the foyer. She hadn't asked about Kyle, she'd see what came of his interview at the station first. She stood waiting for Harry to join her, but there was no sign of him.

"Is there anyone in the office?" she called to Debra.

"Doubt it, love, not with Blackwood laid up."

So where was Harry? She went back inside and collared Edward, who was in the corridor. "You seen my colleague? He was going to the office."

"Nope."

"Mind if I take a look?"

"Help yourself."

Jess didn't need telling twice. She darted down the corridor and ran into Harry, coming the other way. "Find anyone?"

"Apart from Edward, Debra and a couple of waiters, the place is empty," he said. He held up a newspaper. "But I did find this in the office."

"Significant?"

"I hope not. It's a copy of a Glasgow daily and I'm asking myself how it got onto Blackwood's desk."

CHAPTER THIRTY-SEVEN

It was getting late in the day but Harry still had to interview Radford. That would be the biggy, so he decided to speak to Carla first.

"You knew what was going on, how they were getting the heart for Terry. That makes you an accessory to planning a murder," he told her.

"He's my husband. I just want him to live. Is that asking too much?" She looked across the table at him, her eyes blazing. "Radford gave us hope. I didn't ask for any details — truth is, I didn't want to think about them."

"But you knew someone would have to die for Terry to have a chance at life," Harry said.

"Radford told me Dillon was terminally ill and didn't have long to live. He said Dillon had agreed to the operation. I thought Radford was waiting for the lad to die before he took the heart. If I had known . . . well, I honestly don't know how I would have reacted."

She was nothing if not honest. "You'll have to stay with us until I've interviewed Radford," he told her. "If he backs up your story, you'll be able to go home."

Harry returned to the incident room. "Carla says she believed what Radford told her. All she wanted was a new heart for her husband, so she didn't ask how they were going to go about it."

Col handed him a mug of tea. "Radford's solicitor has arrived. He uses Graham Hollis, same as Blackwood."

Harry looked at Jess over the rim of his mug. "You ready for this? It could be a long session."

"No worries. I just want this little lot done with."

Didn't they all. Harry had said nothing more to Jess other than that he'd found a Scottish newspaper in Blackwood's office. But the find bothered him. Who did Blackwood know who'd read a Glasgow paper, and was this the stranger Debra had referred to as 'Scottie'? But the big question was, had this man invested in the clinic? Harry had a bad feeling about him and was hoping that the interview with Radford would put his mind at rest.

* * *

Harry and Jess sat opposite Radford and his solicitor, Hollis, in an interview room. Preliminaries done, Harry said, "Tell me about your investor."

"I can't. He doesn't want anyone to know about our arrangement yet." Radford smiled. "Think of him as a silent partner."

"Is he the foreign surgeon we met?"

"No, but Mr Kozlov is an associate of his."

"Whoever he is, I don't think we can simply take him out of the equation yet." Harry smiled back. "You see, I think it is this silent partner, plus Kozlov, who are instrumental in the transplant surgery." He gave Radford a moment to think about this.

"If this is about that boy Dillon, then you're wrong," Radford said. "He was close to death and we were taking care of him during his final hours. He'd given his full permission for the heart to be transplanted, his kidneys too."

"Close to death," Harry repeated. "I don't think so. Dillon French is currently sitting up in a hospital bed in

Ryebridge General swigging orange juice, with no memory of the last few days. The medics treating him reckon he's been drugged but will be back to full health tomorrow."

"Ryebridge General," Radford scoffed. "What do they know? Dillon is dying, I tell you."

"You're lying. You know damn well the lad is as fit as a fiddle. The only thing wrong with him is a fondness for heroin and a short temper."

"What did you think was wrong with Dillon, Mr Radford?" Jess asked.

"I can't discuss it."

"In that case, back to your investor," Harry said. "Scottish, is he?"

"He is, as it happens," Radford said with a smile. "He's from Glasgow. He's not a medical man, mind, but very good with finance and brilliant at getting hold of what we need at a good price."

"What you need being human organs for your private patients."

Radford stared at Harry for several moments before shaking his head. "You're at it again with your accusations, Inspector. I'm a doctor, a surgeon. I save life, I don't take it."

"But your latest venture is into spare-part surgery, and for that you've taken up with the Scottish villain and the charlatan Kozlov."

"Spare-part surgery is not illegal."

"That depends on where the organs come from," Jess said.

"My investor and Mr Kozlov see to all that and I've never asked for details," he admitted. "What I do know is that we work according to a barter system with other private hospitals. We have an organ we don't intend to use and we swap it for one we need."

"Can I suggest that two corneas and two kidneys have been *bartered* recently?" Harry said.

"I've no idea, I'd have to check the records. Can I go now?"

"No, we've a long way to go before you get out of here. I want the name of your investor, as well as details of your patients and your organ transactions before I even consider it. I also want to know where Blackwood fits into all this."

"He's a louse. Blackwood lent me a percentage of the money I needed to set up the Radford and then bailed. I almost went bankrupt," Radford said angrily. "If it hadn't been for my new investor, there wouldn't be a hospital."

"You and Blackwood fell out?" Harry asked.

"The arrangement was that I'd do his operation and then we'd come to an agreement about what I owed him."

"Did you discuss it with Dillon?" Jess asked coldly. "I bet he'd have had a few things to say on the matter."

"We've discussed this already and I've told you all I know."

"Where does Kyle fit into your *arrangements*?" Jess asked.

"He doesn't. He only started in my employ this week and knows nothing about what goes on." He looked Jess in the eye. "He doesn't even know about the transplants, or my investor, so you needn't waste your time asking him."

"We'll decide what questions we ask," Harry said.

"Well, I can't stay here much longer. I have patients to see to."

"Someone else will have to do that, Mr Radford."

* * *

Kyle was downstairs in reception, waiting for his uncle. Jess was anxious for a word. "What do we do with him?" she asked Harry.

"Tell him to go home but he's not to disappear. We'll probably need another word."

That was fair of Harry. Perhaps he didn't believe Kyle had anything to do with this either.

As soon as she entered the reception area, Kyle stood up. "Can I take Mr Radford back with me?"

"Harry won't let him go yet, and I have to say your uncle isn't helping himself."

"Surely you're not keeping him here overnight?"

"We have no choice, Kyle, and you should think yourself lucky that Harry's willing to let you go." She gave the young man a sideways look. "You are telling the truth, aren't you? You didn't know what was going on — that your uncle was prepared to sacrifice Dillon French's life to save Blackwood's."

"I was led to believe that Dillon was seriously ill. I'd no idea what was really going on. I do what my uncle wants, and in the short time I've been there I've learnt it's not always wise to ask questions."

That was an attitude that needed to change. Jess had a mouthful of abuse ready to throw back at him but held her tongue.

"I don't even know what Uncle Clive is supposed to have done," Kyle said.

"Well, I can't tell you. Go home, Kyle. There's nothing you can do here."

CHAPTER THIRTY-EIGHT

Jess returned to the incident room to find Harry on the phone to Sasha.

"Sash has identified a mobile number that's rung Lansing twice in the last twenty-four hours. It hasn't rung any other time, and he didn't call back. Both calls lasted over three minutes."

"You reckon it's the kidnapper, blackmailer or whatever?"

"I reckon we're getting closer. Are we still keeping an eye on the house?"

"One officer," Col confirmed.

Harry scratched his head. "We need more bodies in the immediate area. Get Bob and Jack to change into plain clothes and park on the road close to Lansing's. He goes out, or any vehicles drive by acting suspicious, we stop them."

It was a breakthrough of sorts in the Lansing case but Jess was only half listening. She stood staring at the incident board. "I've been trying to work out the connection between Lori going missing, Paula's death and all that organ transplant business."

"They have to be connected somehow," Harry said. "Paula's kidneys and eyes were missing, remember."

"That might mean that Lori has fallen foul of these butchers too," Jess said.

Harry shook his head. "I don't think so somehow, but we'll see. We need to find her first. When we do, I've got a number of pertinent questions to ask that lady."

"D'you reckon she was seeing Blackwood?" Jess asked.

"I doubt it now," Harry said. "That's what it might have looked like to the people working at the club, Debra for instance, but Carla would have killed him."

"We're on," Col called across. "The officer we've got watching the Lansings' has just seen a navy-blue van pull up at the end of the road."

Harry grabbed his jacket. "Has the Rainbow had their vans back?"

"Only the clean one," Col replied.

"If it's that one, it has to be someone from the club driving," Jess said.

"I think that's a reasonable assumption," Harry agreed. "Lori often went to the Rainbow. It's not a great leap to assume that whoever she took up with had a connection to the place." He turned to Col. "Make sure our people understand that they must not lose that van whatever happens."

* * *

In less than ten minutes, the pair were pulling into the Lansings' road. Col was on speaker phone, relaying the route taken by the van.

"It waited just long enough for Lansing to put a sports holdall in the back. He didn't speak to whoever was driving, didn't even go round to the front, he went straight back into his house," Col said.

Exactly like before.

"The van is now heading round the park and making its way back to Ryebridge centre."

"Thanks, Col, we're on it," Harry said. "Tell the lads to intercept as soon as they spot a chance."

"Who d'you reckon it is?" Jess asked. "I must say I've got so many names and faces in my head, I can no longer think straight."

Harry gave her a smile. "You're tired, that's all, Jessie. We get this wrapped up and we'll call it a day. We'll finish interviewing Radford in the morning. A night in the cells might make him think."

The two officers in plain clothes had the navy-blue van cornered in a lay-by on the Ryebridge Road. Bob Tait was banging on the driver's door but getting no response.

"It's over," he shouted. "You're not going anywhere, so give up."

The driver simply sat tight, hood up, texting furiously.

Bob tried again. "Come on, open up! Otherwise we'll break down the door and drag you out."

At that moment, Harry and Jess arrived. "Good work," Harry said to Bob. He rapped on the driver's door. "Five minutes with a crowbar and we'll have you in custody. Better all round if you give yourself up." He indicated for Jess to try the rear doors but they, too, were locked.

"It's been a long day and I'm fast running out of patience, so do the sensible thing," he called to the driver.

It was dark and there was little traffic on the road. The van was surrounded, making it impossible for the driver to escape. Eventually the reality of the situation must have hit home. They all heard the click as the lock was released.

Harry reached in, took the phone from the driver's hands, handed it to Jess and pulled back the hood covering the driver's face.

"Well, well, Mrs Lansing. Have you any idea how much trouble and grief you've caused these last weeks?"

Lori Lansing gave Harry a disdainful look. "You're making a mistake. I have friends in high places."

"If that's a threat, it's not a particularly scary one. And if you mean Terry Blackwood, you should know he's at death's door in the Radford."

She shook her head. "Oh no, not Terry. I'm not that desperate."

* * *

Back at the station, Harry flicked on the incident room lights and saw that he and Jess were the last two left. "Col and the others must have gone home. Sorry, Jess, but it looks like it's just you and me. We'll speak to Lori after she's been processed downstairs, but if she wants a solicitor it'll be tomorrow before we can interview her properly."

That'd suit Jess down to the ground. She was tired and wanted to go home. "You didn't seem very surprised to see Lori in that van."

Harry had that look on his face, the one that suggested his instincts had been at it again. "We didn't just get Lori, Jess, the money was in the back, so it's a good result."

"You knew, didn't you?" she said. "Or you suspected. What I don't understand is how."

Harry smiled. "It was a combination of things. I was suspicious when the body turned out to be that of Paula Rushton and not Lori. Then there was what you said about Lansing needing money. I reckoned he could only need that much money for one reason. He'd been contacted again. Whoever her boyfriend is, they plotted to rip off Adam Lansing and disappear together. It wouldn't have been hard to get new identities, not with the people Lori must know through being so close to Blackwood."

"Why didn't Lansing contact us, ask for help?"

"We weren't much help last time, were we? Hewitt got it all wrong. But you're right, we'll have to have a word with Lansing."

Jess sighed. "Do we have to speak to Lori tonight?"

"I'll let her know how serious this is, give her something to ponder on overnight, but we'll leave the hard stuff till tomorrow."

CHAPTER THIRTY-NINE

Saturday

The following morning, Jess and Harry found Lori sitting in an interview room looking decidedly sorry for herself. She had asked for the duty solicitor, who was now at her side and looking as if he'd rather be anywhere else but there.

"I haven't done nothing wrong," she began as soon as she saw them. "I asked Adam for money. So what? He can afford it, not that he'd ever part with it willingly, hence my tactics. And you can't call it blackmail — we were married, so it was as much my money as his."

Harry shook his head. "It's not quite that simple, Lori."

She stuck her nose in the air. "I tell you I've done nothing wrong, and you can't keep me here."

"What have you got to say about Paula Rushton?" Harry asked.

The young woman looked puzzled. "Didn't she die or something? Whatever, it had nothing to do with me."

Harry had no time for this. He wanted straight answers. He'd had enough of her lies, her deceptions. He needed to know what happened and how she was involved. "We want to help you, Lori," he began patiently. "We know Paula died. I want you to tell me how, and what part you played in it."

"It wasn't me, I'm no killer," she protested. She seemed indignant at his suggestion. "Paula had to have some operation or other. That foreign doctor told me there was some sort of medical mishap."

"Believe me, Lori, it was no 'mishap', as you put it. Paula was deliberately murdered. The operation was intended to remove both her kidneys."

Lori's eyes widened. She looked genuinely horrified. "That's not what I was told. Honestly, I believed she'd be fine, and so did Paula. She told me there was no risk. A couple of days in hospital and she'd be back on her feet. She was supposed to get paid for it too."

"Paid for what? As far as we know, Paula didn't need any sort of medical treatment, apart from her weight issues she was a perfectly healthy young woman. So what was this operation supposed to be for?"

Lori sighed. "Paula was selling one of her kidneys. Apparently you can manage with one. The surgeon at the Radford was going to do it. Radford himself assured me that the doctor had a good reputation and she was promised good money for it."

"She was butchered, Lori," Jess said. "Both her kidneys and her eyes were removed and she was left to bleed to death."

Lori broke down. "I'd no idea," she wailed. "If I'd known, I'd have warned her not to go through with it."

"Okay, suppose for a moment we go with what you're telling us. That doesn't explain why her body was mutilated and passed off as yours."

Lori Lansing stopped weeping. "Because it gave me my freedom," she said simply. "Life with Adam is no picnic, believe me. The man is a bully and a control freak."

This description didn't match the man they had met, but then they didn't live with him.

"But you did have your freedom," Jess told her. "You went out, to the Rainbow for instance, and you had friends there."

"I was allowed to go there because I had Terry on my side, and Adam is terrified of crossing him."

"Who helped you, Lori?" Harry asked.

"No one. I did it all on my own."

"Was it you who took a baseball bat to Paula's face and head and rendered her unrecognisable?" he said.

The look of disgust on her face said it all. "No way. That's awful."

"Well, someone did. Then they stuck her in a fridge and when the time was right, dressed her in that Victorian garb belonging to your theatre group and left her body in the park."

Lori looked down.

"The costume was my idea," she finally admitted. "Paula loved it so much I felt it fitting that she should be found wearing it. But I had nothing to do with the rest."

"Did you dress her yourself?" Jess asked.

Lori Lansing stared at the pair. "No, I gave the outfit to someone else who dressed her in it. I thought she'd died because of something that went wrong during the op. She was wearing a hospital gown. I didn't want her buried in that."

Harry was losing patience. "I need a name, Lori."

She started to weep again. "This wasn't supposed to happen. I was promised it all would work out and we'd be able to go away together and leave it all behind."

"Who? Who promised you?" Jess asked.

"The man I love," Lori said simply. "He's as trapped as me in his own way. I'm stifled by Adam, he by his family. We talked long and hard about what to do, how to get out, then Terry gave us a way to do it."

"Terry Blackwood helped you? Did he kill Paula?"

"No, but he knew she was dead. Radford told him, I think. He told me and my fella that there was a body at the clinic that had to be got rid of. I had no idea it was Paula. I should have joined the dots but I didn't. I just grabbed the chance. The three of us came up with a plan that'd give us everything we needed. I'd pretend to have been abducted, get the money off Adam, and then we'd dump the body. Terry was going to make sure everyone would think it was me. He said he'd deal with the DNA that was bound to be requested and all I had to do was keep a low profile."

"But you got greedy," Harry said.

"Terry is dying, there is a new team running both the club and that clinic. The new boss knows what we did and he threatened us. He's not a man you cross and we needed to get away fast. We couldn't take any risks. I sent Adam a video clip of me as proof that I was still alive, and asked for more money." She glanced up. "As you know, he paid up."

"He had to sell his Ryebridge store to raise the money," Jess told her. "It was the first one he ever opened and it meant a lot to him."

"I'm not proud of what I've done, but I was desperate for a way out," Lori said. "Does he hate me?"

"Not yet," Harry said. "But that might change when he finds out it was you that ruined him."

"I am sorry. I only wanted to be free."

"Who helped you, Lori? Who are you running away with?"

But she remained tight-lipped. "I can't say."

"We will find out. With DNA and what witnesses tell us, we'll get a name eventually. But things will go easier for you if you tell us now."

She gave a heartfelt sigh and turned towards the window. "I do love him, you know. All I wanted was for us to be happy."

"His name, Lori."

"Kyle Stanton."

CHAPTER FORTY

Jess staggered back to the incident room, her head reeling. "I can't believe it. It can't be Kyle. Yes, he goes to the Rainbow, it was him who first took me, but he doesn't know the staff there nor they him. He doesn't even know David Parsons, the manager."

"Lori named him, Jess," Harry said. "Why would she lie? After all, it's in her interest to tell us the truth. She's in a lot of trouble, she's an accessory to murder and she's realised her best bet is to tell us the truth. Kyle is obviously not as innocent as you thought. I need to bring him in, find out what he knows and determine his part in all this." He'd made a pot of tea and handed Jess a mug. "Didn't you ever suspect that there was something dodgy about the bloke?"

"No, not for one minute. You did, though, didn't you? You asked me about him, remember."

"Yes, but I didn't have him down as the man Lori Lansing was involved with. Since it would appear that he is, you can no longer be involved. I'm sorry."

Fair enough. She and Kyle were friends, and up until today, she thought they'd been getting closer. "What are we doing about Paula?"

"I want to know who killed her. Although I have a shrewd idea."

"Not Radford, surely? He's a surgeon, he's supposed to save lives. Kozlov, perhaps? Radford's new helpmate."

"It's a strong possibility but there is someone else involved in all this, Jess. They're involved in both Paula's death and what's happening at the clinic. I believe Kozlov did the surgery and this other person wanted her finished off, told Kozlov to harvest her kidneys and eyes."

"Blackwood. How involved d'you think he was?" she asked.

"Before he became ill, I reckon he knew enough."

"So who are we looking at now? There are no more names in the mix."

Harry shook his head and picked up the Glasgow newspaper from his desk. "There is one, Jess, but I really hope I'm wrong."

Jess couldn't think beyond Kyle's involvement and didn't pursue his comment. She wrote it off as simply another example of Harry's obsession with Glasgow gangland. "You go after Kyle and I'll take Col and have a word with Lansing."

Harry nodded. "Make sure he understands that he should have informed us of this new demand for money."

* * *

When Adam Lansing opened the door to them, he asked no questions. He simply stood aside, invited them in and closed the door.

"I'm expecting Lori back at any moment. The people who took her may be watching the house, so be quick."

"No one is watching, Mr Lansing," Jess said. "And Lori will be a while yet. We have her down at the station."

His face broke into a delighted smile. "You found her? They let her go?"

"No, we arrested her," Jess said. The poor man still hadn't realised that he'd been duped. "Lori is behind the whole thing. She made up the entire kidnap scam to extort money from you."

The look on his face said it all. It was too hard for him to accept. "No! Never. My Lori would never do that to me."

"I'm afraid she did, and she's got herself involved in a whole lot more besides," Jess said.

Adam Lansing stumbled as he led the way into the sitting room. He sat down hard. "Why? I'd have given her the money. She had only to ask, she must know that."

"The person that rang," Col asked, "the one that made the demands, was the voice a man's or a woman's?"

"Male. No doubt about it."

"You're sure? They didn't use a voice changer to alter the tone or depth?"

"Look, young man, I can tell the difference between a male voice and a female's, and it was definitely male. Deep, raspy, and I got the impression he was trying to hide an accent."

Jess looked at Col. Whoever Lori had persuaded to make those calls, it wasn't Blackwood. He'd worked on his accent over the years and it was now quite plummy.

"I assume you were convinced that Lori was still alive, or you wouldn't have parted with the money," Jess said.

"They sent me a video clip of her. It was Lori all right, no doubt about it. They filmed her in front of a TV which was showing that day's news. That's all I needed. I raised the money and this time I followed their instructions to the letter, which is why I didn't contact you lot. Last time you let me down and I lost her."

"Mr Lansing, Lori was playing games with you. Quite possibly fleecing you twice was always part of her plan."

He sat, head down, a broken man. "Will she come back, do you think?"

"I'm not sure," Jess said. "She extorted money and we have the body of a murdered woman in the morgue. Your wife needs to tell us exactly what happened to her and who was involved before we can consider allowing her to come home."

"Can I see her?" Lansing asked.

"Possibly. We'll let you know."

"She'll need a good solicitor. I'll get her one and ask him to go to the station straight away. Tell Lori I have her back and that I'm doing my best for her."

Jess was amazed. What he'd just said was beyond her comprehension. His wife had bled him dry but still he stood firmly in her corner.

* * *

Harry had sent two uniformed officers to fetch Kyle, who now sat in an interview room looking decidedly edgy. Harry watched him through the two-way window, trying to make up his mind about him. Was he guilty or not? Still undecided, Harry went in to confront him.

"Morning, Kyle. Thanks for making yourself available. I'll try not to keep you long. This is simply an informal chat to get things straight."

"Is this about my uncle?" Kyle asked.

"No, Kyle, it's about Lori Lansing." Harry paused, waiting for a reaction. "You know, the woman you plotted with to extort money from her husband before you both planned to disappear."

Kyle looked genuinely bemused, nothing like a crook who'd been found out.

"I've no idea what you're on about," he said at last. "I don't even know the woman, never mind planning to run off with her."

"Lori has told us all about it and she's named you. What you did, the money you both took from her husband and how Paula got caught up in it all and ended up dead."

Kyle now appeared to be totally confused. He looked at Harry as if he'd lost his mind. "This is rubbish. Who told you these lies? Where did they come from?"

"As I said. Lori."

"I don't know what her game is, whoever she is, but she's got it all wrong. I had nothing to do with her or what was going on at the clinic."

"But you do work there, and you do frequent the Rainbow."

"Yes, I do work at the clinic but I don't know everything that goes on there. I've only been in the post a week, for heaven's sake. As for the Rainbow, it's the only bit of nightlife in this town. Besides, I needed somewhere decent to take Jess. She's the first girl I've met since moving here three weeks ago, so I haven't had time to look for another respectable eatery."

"Three weeks? That all? Where were you before, then?" Harry asked, surprised.

"Cornwall. I worked in insurance, in St Austell. I rented a little cottage in the nearby village of Luxulyan. The area is lovely but it doesn't offer what I'm looking for. My uncle Clive created the post in his clinic specially for me. Thanks to him, I had a chance to earn some real money and save for a deposit on a house of my own. It gave me a foothold on the ladder. Some progress!" he said bitterly. "I haven't been here a month and you lot have me down as an accessory to murder."

CHAPTER FORTY-ONE

Harry returned to the incident room and slammed the file down on the nearest desk. "She lied. What Lori told us about Kyle Stanton was completely untrue." He looked at Col, who'd just returned with Jess. "Get onto our colleagues in St Austell. I want everything you can find about Kyle, just to make sure."

Jess smiled. "I knew he was innocent."

"He hasn't lived around here long enough for him to be guilty of any of it," Harry said.

"Adam Lansing wasn't any help either. He still wants her back," Jess said.

"I doubt she'll want to go. It's obvious that Lori is protecting someone."

The big question was who. Blackwood seemed an unlikely candidate. When Harry had told Lori how ill he was, she didn't appear all that concerned. "We can probably rule out Kyle, Blackwood too, so who does that leave us?"

"Among the crew at the Rainbow, hardly anyone," Jess said.

She was sitting at her desk in front of a mountain of paperwork. "Debra might know. She's been a great pair of eyes and ears on that place." She picked up her mobile and rang her. "We need your help. We've found Lori — safe and well incidentally — but we need to know who she was seeing."

"It's early," Debra complained. "A girl needs her beauty sleep and I'm injured, remember."

"Sorry, I wouldn't bother you if it wasn't important."

"I already told you, Terry Blackwood," Debra said.

"Yes, but are you sure there was no one else? For example, did she ever show an interest in that young man you've seen me with, Kyle?"

"I doubt their paths ever crossed. Lori was well missing by the time he first showed up."

"Think carefully, Debra. Is there anyone else, someone she spoke to you about?"

"As far as blokes at the club went, she didn't go for any of those security-guard types. And apart from Dave, there isn't anyone else."

"David Parsons?" Jess asked.

"He's a bit of a nerd, but Lori likes that in a man."

That got Jess thinking. Could Lori and David be an item? Could he really have done those things for money? She thought back to their schooldays. He'd been bullied, branded a softie, always the butt of the latest jokes and hadn't made friends easily. But he'd come through it and was now on Blackwood's payroll. "Thanks. You've been a great help."

"We'll speak to Lori again," she told Harry. "Tell her we know about David Parsons and see where it goes."

"Parsons? Are you sure?"

"No, but he was the only name Debra could come up with."

"Is that solicitor here, the one her husband promised to get for her?" Harry asked.

"Downstairs," Bob Tait said.

"Good, because this time we'll be interviewing Lori under caution."

* * *

195

Formalities over, Harry gave Lori a smile. "I hope we made you comfortable overnight."

"I want to go. You can't keep me here. I've told you everything I know."

"Not quite. We still don't have the name of the man who helped you, the one you planned to abscond with," Harry said.

"I told you, Kyle Stanton. Speak to him, he's not hard to find."

"We have done, Lori, and he's not the one. For starters, he wasn't even living in Ryebridge when Paula was killed."

"So? That means nothing."

"David Parsons, on the other hand, was, and he's a friend of yours."

Lori's head shot up and she fixed her eyes on Harry's. "No. Leave David out of this. He's a good man, none of it's his fault."

"None of what, Lori? The murder of Paula and scamming your husband out of a fortune?"

Lori turned to her solicitor. "I don't like the way this is going. I want this to stop. I just want to go home and make peace with my husband."

"D'you have any actual evidence that my client is guilty of anything?" the solicitor asked.

"The two of us caught her red-handed after she'd just picked up the money from Lansing's house," Harry said. "Plus, she had access to the clothing the dead girl was found in."

The solicitor whispered in Lori's ear for several seconds.

"He says I should tell you everything, and if I do that I'll get bail." Though Lori didn't seem very impressed by this advice, she took a deep breath and began to talk. "It began as a joke one night. David thought the way Adam treated me was unfair, particularly since I didn't have access to any money of my own. He said we should fix it. He said that if Adam believed that I'd been kidnapped, he'd pay up. At that point, it was just idle talk over a bottle of wine in the club one night."

"And Paula?" Harry asked.

"I'm not lying, I really didn't have anything to do with that. I thought she was an idiot for even considering selling a kidney, and I told her so. But Paula wouldn't have it. She told me they were paying her ten grand and that she needed the cash."

"Who was paying her?" Harry asked.

"Them up at the clinic. Radford and that Scottish chap, the weird one with the scar on his face."

Jess glanced at Harry to see if this rang any bells. He was the expert in Scottish villains. She looked again. Harry appeared to be in shock. His face was deathly pale and his hands were shaking. She nudged him under the table and whispered, "You okay?"

Harry shook his head and rose from his seat. "Sorry, I don't feel very well."

He sprinted down the corridor and into the toilet, where he threw up. He knew who she meant. He knew only too well. Mungo Salton's face was etched into his mind as deeply as the scar he wore. His old enemy was here, in Ryebridge. But why?

CHAPTER FORTY-TWO

Harry was back in the incident room when Jess came in. "Lori's solicitor is banging on about bail," she told him.

"Okay," he said. "But I want her to check in on a daily basis. She does a runner and she'll be back inside."

"What about David Parsons?"

"Send a couple of uniformed officers to the Rainbow to bring him in," Harry said.

She looked at his grey face. "What was it, something you ate or what Lori said about the Scotsman at the club?"

"I think it's Salton," he said simply. "The description fits, I mean, who else has a scar like that?"

"What's he up to?" she asked.

"I've no idea but I intend to find out. We'll speak to Parsons and get his take on the changes taking place in Blackwood's organisation," Harry said.

"Don't you think we should find out how Blackwood is? If he's feeling any better, he may be able to help us."

"I doubt he'd do anything so public-spirited, Jessie. Let's get our chat with Parsons done with and then we'll decide how to deal with the new regime at the Rainbow."

* * *

David Parsons obviously wasn't happy to have been brought in. He was sitting in the interview room with the duty solicitor and Harry. He'd been cautioned, and his prints and DNA sample taken.

"Certain people will take a dim view of this," he said to Harry. "Life at the club is difficult enough without bringing down Mungo's wrath on my head."

"Mungo Salton?"

Parsons nodded. "He told me he knew you. Said you had unfinished business."

True, but not something Harry wanted to discuss right now. "Paula Rushton. What happened to her?"

"I speak to you and Salton will cut out my tongue and make me eat it."

Parsons was deadly serious. In the short time he must have known Salton, he'd evidently got the true measure of the man.

"I know what a fiend he is." Harry held up his hands in front of Parson's face. "I crossed him once and I got this for my trouble."

Parsons winced. "I'm not telling you anything, and you can't make me."

"But I can charge you with murder. That fails, there's being an accessory to murder. You'll go down. D'you want that, David? Or would you rather tell me the truth?"

David Parsons was silent, considering his options, Harry hoped.

"What about Lori?"

"She extorted money from her husband and planned to abscond with it," Harry said. "He thought she was dead."

"Salton needs stopping," Parsons said, "but I can't help you. Mungo Salton is a one-man killing machine without a conscience. There's no way I'm telling you anything."

Harry smiled. "You don't have a police record, so we didn't have your DNA in our files. But we have it now, along with a number of samples taken during our investigations that we're still waiting to identify. For example, are you a Ryebridge Celtic supporter? Lost your club badge recently?"

Harry watched Parsons's face fall. He realised the consequences of this only too well.

"We found a Celtic badge, David. It was snatched from the man who attacked Debra Dobson in that alleyway. What are the chances that the unknown DNA on it will be a match for yours?"

"You're lying. You must be, I've been so careful."

"You will stay with us until the results are in. When they are, we'll talk again."

Harry left the room and went off to find Jess.

* * *

"Parsons is as guilty as sin," he said straight off. "But he won't talk, not yet. He's too scared of Salton."

"We're keeping him then," she said.

"Until the DNA results are in. They are something he can't refute. Meanwhile, we interview Radford again, see what we can get from him."

Harry sat down in the incident room and gulped down a glass of water. He felt dreadful, but with everything going on, he couldn't call it a day.

Col held out the phone. "Melanie, boss."

"You were right," she confirmed. "The body in the park, the woman in the strange garb, was Paula Rushton. I'm still working on the unknown DNA, testing it against that of David Parsons. You'll have to give me a bit longer for that. Now for the interesting bit. Among the many different samples we found in Paula's flat, we found one belonging to a villain from Glasgow, one Callum Muir. He belongs to a gang run by someone called Mungo Salton."

"He was in Paula's flat?"

"Yes. We found his DNA on a bag containing crack cocaine stashed under the sofa."

Proof, if he needed it, that Salton was taking over the dealing in the town. "Any tie-up with Wilson's death?"

"Yes. Wilson must have lashed out, scratched his attacker and drawn blood. We found some on his clothing, extracted the DNA, and that too belongs to Muir."

This was good news, scary but good. Harry now had evidence against one of Salton's mob. If the lad would talk to him, agree to give evidence, then he could nail Salton once and for all.

"What d'you want to do?" Jess asked. "Given how dangerous this Salton is, we could ask for Armed Response."

Harry shook his head. "Salton hasn't threatened us. We have no evidence against him personally, but we'll go to the Rainbow and arrest this man, Muir."

"There'll be trouble. From what little you've told me about Mungo Salton, he won't like it," Jess said.

"Too bad, it's what we're going to do. But first we'll interview Radford, see what he's got to say for himself. We'll also bring in the surgeon, Kozlov." He looked at Col. "Get up to that clinic and sort it."

CHAPTER FORTY-THREE

Radford was sitting with Graham Hollis, the solicitor. He'd been cautioned and looked grey and ill with worry.

"What happened?" Harry began. "How did you get involved with a man like Mungo Salton and his crew?"

Radford winced at the sound of the name. "I don't know who you're talking about."

Despite all that had happened, he was still holding out. "Yes, you do. He's your secret investor, isn't he? He came along, money no object, and promised you everything on your wish list, namely your own clinic. The problem was, Clive, that in return you'd have to do exactly what Salton wanted. And from what I know of you, I can't believe that was at all palatable."

Clive Radford lowered his head and stared at his hands. "I had no choice. The man's an animal, he has no morals. He intends to use my clinic as his latest money-making venture, staff it with the right people and offer an exclusive service." Radford cleared his throat. "Exclusive and toxic. Murder the lost and unwanted and use their organs to feed a steady stream of the unscrupulous unwell."

"And you were going to let this happen? You were going to give in, take orders and go along with this abomination?" Harry looked at him in disgust.

"It wasn't that simple," Radford bleated. "I needed the money and I'd exhausted all the other avenues. The bank won't help, I'm in debt to Blackwood, I had nowhere else to go. Then, just when I believed all was lost, Salton showed up."

All a bit neat and Harry was curious. "What caused him to come here and meet you? How did that happen? Ryebridge isn't exactly a prime location."

"I've no idea why he's here, but it was Blackwood who introduced us. One evening Salton arrived at that club of Blackwood's, they swapped a few words and then he moved into the flat upstairs. I got the impression they'd struck some sort of deal a while ago. Within the week, Salton and he made me an offer."

"What did Blackwood get out of the deal?" Harry asked.

"His transplant. I was to carry out the operation. Blackwood said he had a donor lined up, he'd sort the details and I had nothing to worry about. His only stipulation was that I was not to discuss it with anyone. I met the young lad, the donor, and knew at once that it was all wrong. But Blackwood insisted we went ahead, said he'd get rid of the body and I wasn't to ask questions."

"The donor was Dillon French."

Radford nodded. "And I did question what we were doing. I had a real go at Blackwood. Told him that I'm a doctor, a surgeon, that my role is to save lives, not take them. Blackwood went straight to Salton and me and my family were threatened. What was I supposed to do?"

"You could have come to us," Harry said.

"I was told not to speak to the police, you in particular."

That had to be Salton's decision. But Harry was no further forward in finding out what had brought Salton to Ryebridge in the first place. Harry had been careful. As far as he was aware, there was no way Salton could have found him by accident. Someone must have alerted him, but who? It was vital that this question be answered or he'd never be safe. He had to find out who'd blown his cover.

"Why here? Why did Salton stumble on this particular town?" he said.

Radford hung his head. "He didn't. Blackwood told him. From the few scraps of conversation I overheard, you were the bait. They have a mutual acquaintance among the Glasgow villains. Your name came up by accident, at least that's what Blackwood told me. It was all the incentive Salton needed, it seems. As for the clinic, that was a bonus. Spare-part surgery is extremely lucrative, it's a venture Salton has moved into up in Glasgow. He asked Blackwood to identify a private clinic they could use here, along with a surgeon. When we first met him I assumed he was a regular business-man. It wasn't until it became clear what his real aim for the clinic was that I realised I'd been duped. By then it was too late, I owed a lot of money and had no way to pay it back. Salton promised he'd fix all that."

"And Kozlov?"

"He's Salton's man, works in the Glasgow clinic. He's a vicious bastard who doesn't give a damn for human life." Radford wiped a tear from his eye. "I was present when he harvested the kidneys from that poor girl. Once he'd fin-ished, he severed both renal arteries like they were bits of string. He didn't give a damn, just stood by and watched her bleed out."

"What're Blackwood's chances of survival?" Jess asked.

"Not good," Radford said. "There's little to be done at this stage. He's had heart problems for a while and despite trying hard to keep healthy, he collapsed with a massive heart attack the other day. I doubt he'll recover."

Harry had heard enough. They needed to find Salton and bring him in. He took hold of the file and stood up. "I want you to stay here," he told Radford. "You'll be safer with us for the next day or so. We need to get Salton and his crew rounded up before we even think about bail. Salton has even a slight suspicion you've spoken to me and he'll kill you."

"Can I remind you that my client has patients who need him. He didn't kill anybody," Hollis said. "He was coerced into being a party to what occurred."

"Right now I'm more concerned for his safety," Harry said. "The file will be passed on to the CPS and they will decide what charges he should answer to."

CHAPTER FORTY-FOUR

Harry and Jess returned to the incident room, where they found Bob Tait busy at a workstation. "Is Col having any luck finding Kozlov?" Harry asked.

"He's been up to the clinic but Kozlov's not there," Bob said. "He rang in to say he was trying the club next."

Harry took his mobile from his pocket and rang Col. Right now, he didn't want his colleague anywhere near that club, not without backup and not with Salton around. But Col didn't pick up. Harry had no alternative but to organise the troops to go after him. Salton was dangerous and he couldn't risk Col running into him.

"Organise half a dozen men to come with me to the Rainbow," he told Bob. He picked up the phone to call Rodders. "And just in case, I'll have a word with the super, get him to alert Armed Response in case we have a situation."

"If you're going to the club, I'm coming too," Jess told him. "It's about time I met this Mungo Salton. I want to see this man you're up against for myself."

"I'd rather you didn't, Jess. Salton hates me. He blames me for the death of his son and has sworn to get even. He won't rest until I'm dead, as well as those I'm close to. You and the others are the nearest thing to family I've got down here. He won't hesitate to do you harm, and he has no love of the police either. He lays eyes on you, my work partner, and you'll be the perfect target."

"In that case, you need all the help you can get. And that includes me."

"Okay, but no heroics."

Jess smiled. "As I keep telling people, I'm not the heroic type."

* * *

Col screamed out in pain. Salton's sharp punch to the guts left him sick and disorientated. He raised his head, blood dripping from his nose — a blow inflicted by one of Salton's crew who'd head-butted him while he was being seized.

The man with the Scottish accent breathed in his ear. "Nothing personal, laddie. Look at it from my point of view. I've come a long way and invested a lot of money in getting my hands on the murdering liar who wrecked my life. And what happens? I get delayed by stupid folk who won't talk to me. I'm running out of patience. I don't find Lennox soon, the lot of you will suffer."

Col knew about the beef between this man and Harry but he didn't know the cause. There was certainly a great deal of hate on both sides. He spat out a gob of blood and gasped out, "You're making a big mistake. I'm warning you, Harry will come here and finish you."

This made Mungo Salton laugh. "I'm counting on it, laddie, and I'll be waiting." He turned to the man standing behind him. "Callum, put him somewhere safe until I can deal with him." He laughed again. "And don't make him too comfortable."

"Callum Muir?" Col breathed. "We've a warrant out for your arrest too. Think hard about what you do next, who you side with."

Ignoring the warning, Callum took hold of Col and manhandled him towards the cellar door. Opening it wide, he kicked Col down the stone steps.

"Get the lads ready," Salton told Muir. "The police come here, we'll give them a welcome they won't forget." Salton swaggered past the bar, where in terrified silence, the staff were cleaning up after the night before. None of them dared to even glance his way. This one was nothing like Blackwood. At least he treated his staff with some semblance of decency. This one was brutal, far too handy with his fists. The only one of Blackwood's staff he had any interaction with, or time for, was Debra.

Salton helped himself to a whisky and stood leaning against the bar.

Edward approached him. "The brewery has been on the phone, sir. They want a call back with the order for next week."

"Tell them to go to hell," Salton growled. "And you lot might as well pack up and leave. This place is closing as from now."

"Sorry, sir, you can't do that. Mr Blackwood wouldn't like it."

Salton stared at Edward, his eyes glinting with rage. This wasn't the way his staff spoke to him. He strode around the bar to confront him, but the bear of a man stood his ground.

"I promised Mr Blackwood I'd keep this place ticking over until he got back," he said.

"Kozlov!" Salton shouted. "I've got another one for you."

The surgeon was in a far corner, hunched over a brandy. He approached the burly guard and ran his eyes up and down his body. "Keep fit, do you?" He poked him in the stomach. "Hard as metal, you obviously eat well too. You'll make a good specimen."

Salton had a grin on his face and it didn't suit him. "My doctor friend here will fillet you good and serve you up as spare parts. Let's hear you plead Blackwood's case then."

Edward reached out, grabbed Kozlov by the scruff of his neck and threw him across the room. He turned back to Salton. "I won't be threatened. You'd do well to remember that. You're a fool if you think you can get away with what you're doing."

Salton smiled back. "Oh, but I will get away with it. You see, there is nothing anyone can do to stop me."

Salton glanced down at Kozlov, writhing on the floor and groaning in pain.

"The brute has broken my ribs," he cried out.

Salton was having none of it. "Get to your feet. There's work to do."

The few seconds Salton's attention was off him was all Edward needed. He took his pistol from his inside coat pocket and held it against Salton's neck. "Don't try anything," he threatened. "Do not speak or move unless I tell you."

CHAPTER FORTY-FIVE

Not having sufficient officers at his own station, Harry put out a call to Ashton and they had men on the way. Along with Armed Response on standby, they were now ready to go.

Jess and Harry parked outside the Rainbow, a second car behind. Jess said, "We should wait for the others, it's too dangerous to go it alone."

But Harry was too impatient. Col was inside the club and, knowing Salton, probably desperate for their help. "You wait here for the rest of the backup. I have to go in now, Col's life might depend on it." He leaped out of the car.

"No!" Jess shouted. "We do this together, all of us. We storm the place, go inside mob-handed and take them off-guard. Then you can take advantage of the mayhem to grab Salton and slap handcuffs on him."

Harry could see she wasn't in any mood to argue. He beckoned the other officers forward and tried the main entrance doors, fully expecting them to be locked. They weren't.

"Go careful, now" he said. "We've no idea what we're walking into."

"And Salton doesn't know we're coming," Jess said.

Inside, the main bar area was dimly lit. It looked empty but the hairs on the back of Harry's neck were prickling. Something was wrong.

"I've been waiting a long time for this moment." Harry would have recognised that thick Glaswegian accent anywhere. "And I'm not a patient man."

There he was in front of him, large as life, the man Harry had been running from these last couple of years. He looked the same — the heavy build, that scar down his cheek — but his eyes, the way they stared at him, that wasn't the same. The deadly hate in them was something new.

"I'm here to bring you in, Salton," Harry said.

Salton gave a throaty laugh. "I could shoot you down where you stand. The only reason I'm holding back is because I want you to suffer first."

Harry took a step backward. "This has to end now."

"Call off your people," Salton ordered. "If you don't, my men will pick them off one by one, starting with the little lady there."

Harry chanced a backward glance and saw Jess standing a couple of metres behind him. "You won't get away with this. We've got armed officers on the way."

Salton laughed more loudly. "By the time they get here, we'll be long gone, and you, Lennox, will have breathed your last."

Harry took a swift look at his surroundings. Salton was standing by a window whose blinds were down, so he was partially in shadow. As he scanned the area between them, Harry saw the shape of a man lying by the bar. From the size of him, it had to be Edward. "What have you done to him?"

"He threatened me, he even had the gall to pull a gun. Sorry, Lennox, but people don't do that to me, not even giants like him."

"He's not dead, is he?"

"What d'you think? I'm a good shot and he's a big target."

Harry made a move to go to Edward but Salton shot at his feet, sending him scuttling backwards.

"Stay where you are," Salton ordered.

"At least let me check if he's still alive," Harry said.

Salton moved towards Edward and kicked at his back. There was a dull thud, Edward didn't even groan. "He's a gonner. Anyway, I've got better things to do than stand here talking to you." Salton aimed his pistol at Harry and fired. The shot hit him in the upper arm. It caught Harry off-balance. He screamed and staggered backwards.

Salton roared with laughter. He called out to his men. "Get in here. Put the others somewhere while I play with Mr Detective here." He fired another shot at Harry's leg but this time Harry was ready. He swerved to the side, got down on the floor and rolled over to Edward. He heard Salton's men enter the room and gestured for Jess and the others to keep their distance.

"Not good enough, Lennox. There's no escape," Salton growled.

Harry's arm was on fire, the wound bleeding freely, but there was nothing he could do about that. A second shot rang out and Harry heard Bob Tait swear. "Get down!" he screamed at his people.

More laughter from Salton. Harry heard the tramp of heavy footsteps and looked up to see a grinning Salton standing over him, pistol aimed at his head. "The game's just got boring, Lennox. Time to finish it, once and for all."

Harry closed his eyes. The game was indeed over. He'd reached the end of the line. He felt the gun barrel cold against his temple and held his breath. Somewhere in the distance, Jess was screaming. He wanted desperately to help her, but there was nothing he could do.

A shot rang out. Harry blinked. How come he was still alive? Was Salton still playing with him? He turned his head and saw his old enemy lying still beside him. There was blood everywhere.

"He deserved to die, he was an evil man," Edward said. "He ruined Mr Blackwood's life and made him ill. The man had no respect for anyone. All he knew was violence."

This could not be real. Was he in limbo or whatever they called it? Suddenly Jess was beside him, fussing over his arm. The place was full of armed response officers. A little late, but they still had Salton's men to deal with.

Edward struggled to his feet, went to the bar and poured two large whiskies. "Two of his men are in the cellar with your officer, he may need your help. The others are in the back."

Harry gestured to the others. "Bring them up." He took a glass from Edward and swallowed the whisky in one. "I owe you my life. Your brave actions have saved me and my colleagues."

"Kozlov is hiding upstairs with Salton's thugs, nursing his wounds. He too is an evil man."

"Edward, where did you get the gun from?" Jess asked.

"I need it for the job. People don't argue with a gun, and luckily I was carrying two." He looked at Harry. "Just as well for you that I was. I threatened Salton with my small pistol and he knocked it out of my hand and floored me. What he didn't know was that I also had Mr Blackwood's gun. When the boss became ill he asked me to put it in the safe, but I forgot and it was still in my coat pocket."

As he was speaking, Col staggered into the room. He looked dreadful, his head covered in blood from when he'd been thrown down the stone stairs. "There were two of them down there with me," he told Harry. "Vicious buggers, the pair of 'em. One of them is Callum Muir."

Time to wind this up. Harry's arm hurt like hell and he felt weak from loss of blood. Callum also needed seeing to. Harry gestured to the others to cuff Salton's men and get them into the vans waiting to receive them.

"There's a whole fleet of ambulances outside," Jess said. "I reckon we need to get you, Col and Edward shipped off to the hospital as soon as. That arm of yours looks bad."

"Without Edward, I'd have a bullet in my brain." Harry struggled to his feet. "How d'you feel?" he asked the big man.

"I'll live, don't worry about me. I'll get a taxi and go visit Mr Blackwood, tell him what's happened."

"We'll need a statement later," Harry told him.

Jess helped Harry to a waiting ambulance. "What'll happen to Edward?" she asked. "He did have two guns on him and he killed Salton."

"Just as well he had them, isn't it? I'm sure the powers that be will go easy once they know the facts," Harry said.

"You're going to need some time off," Jess said. "You and Col are both going to be laid up for a while."

"Kozlov and Muir need interviewing, and don't forget the forensic results from Hettie. We need them for proof."

"I know, I know, don't go on. I want to nail David Parsons. I reckon it was him who attacked Debra," she said.

"Don't jump to conclusions. Wait for Hettie, and if the hospital do keep me in, I want regular updates, mind."

EPILOGUE

"I'm not that keen on grapes," Harry said, picking at the bunch.

"You're lucky to get anything, the amount of work you've put our way this last week or so," Hettie said. "Well, if you don't like grapes, what do you want?"

"Chocolate."

Hettie grinned. "Chocolate. You're nothing but a big soft girl, Harry Lennox. Anyway, down to business. We finally have the forensic proof that the woman's body is Paula Rushton."

Harry grunted. "Better late than never."

"The football badge had Parson's DNA on it, along with the evidence bag the toothbrush was delivered in, so you can tick him off too."

This was all good news, pity he had to hear it in a hospital bed. He looked up as Jess joined the pair of them. She plonked a carrier bag down beside him and grabbed a chair. He smiled. "You've got your evidence against Parsons then."

"Oh yes, and he's coughed. He attacked Debra because he was convinced she knew about Paula and had told us, but of course she didn't. All along she thought it was Lori who'd gone missing," Jess said.

Hettie smiled. "I haven't told him the best bit yet."

Jess gave him a big grin. "You are going to love this."

"The blood we found on Jamie Wilson's clothing wasn't his," Hettie said. "There was a match to Callum Muir, but since then we've had a look at Salton's body and we found a tiny amount of blood on his jacket that belonged to Wilson."

"In that case, he must have had a hand in Wilson's murder," Harry said.

"The lad was shot in the head and some of his blood spattered Salton and Muir."

Harry smiled. "Shame the man's dead, I'd like to have charged him."

"Blackwood is clinging on," Jess said. "Radford's got another specialist to run the clinic and he's trialling a new drug. He does know he has questions to answer. The files we compiled on Radford, Blackwood, Lori and the others have gone to the CPS and we're waiting to hear back."

Harry lay back against his pillow. "Shame I didn't see it from the start. All that time spent going after Blackwood, when all the time he was the wrong man. It's my own fault for not looking further afield."

"When are you getting out?" Hettie asked.

"I'd be home now if the damned bullet hadn't got lodged against a bone." He winced. "But I'm recovering well from the op. A bit of physio and I'll be as good as new."

"What then? Back to work?" Jess asked. "We'll let you take it easy. I'll even help you find a place of your own if you like."

"We'll see," he said, noncommittally.

"I know why Ryan got rid of you too," she said. "Salton paid him, he even threatened his family back in Scotland. I tell you, Harry, that's one man the world won't miss."

Harry had an odd look on his face. "I'm not sure what I'm going to do, Jessie. With Salton gone, all that prevented me from going home has gone with him. I've got some serious thinking to do."

Jess pulled a face. "You know we don't want to lose you."

Harry saw from her face that she meant it, and he was grateful. Still undecided, he said, "I'll sleep on it. I'll go home for a break when I'm better. If I think I can fit back in, pick up the threads of my old life, then who knows?"

THE END

THE JOFFE BOOKS STORY

We began in 2014 when Jasper agreed to publish his mum's much-rejected romance novel and it became a bestseller.

Since then we've grown into the largest independent publisher in the UK. We're extremely proud to publish some of the very best writers in the world, including Joy Ellis, Faith Martin, Caro Ramsay, Helen Forrester, Simon Brett and Robert Goddard. Everyone at Joffe Books loves reading and we never forget that it all begins with the magic of an author telling a story.

We are proud to publish talented first-time authors, as well as established writers whose books we love introducing to a new generation of readers.

We have been shortlisted for Independent Publisher of the Year at the British Book Awards three times, in 2020, 2021 and 2022, and for the Diversity and Inclusivity Award at the Independent Publishing Awards in 2022.

We built this company with your help, and we love to hear from you, so please email us about absolutely anything bookish at: feedback@joffebooks.com.

If you want to receive free books every Friday and hear about all our new releases, join our mailing list: www.joffebooks. com/contact

And when you tell your friends about us, just remember: it's pronounced Joffe as in coffee or toffee!